"We've talked ... evening," said

Lisa smiled. "I agree.

She'd had him figured out since day one. He'd been hell-bent on endearing himself to her, making himself indispensable, and truth be told, she didn't mind that much. She needed the experience he had to offer. But his ruse was so transparent, she'd have to be blindfolded in a dark room not to see it.

His surprise at the sexy transformation was gratifying. More than gratifying. *Delicious.* She'd caught him off guard. Turned the tables on Mr. Cool. She was sure he'd intended to impress her with the expensive wine and dinner. But he'd been expecting to impress and win over the Lisa with the baggy clothing and bad hair—not this new and improved version.

She smiled to herself. Maybe he'd just have to try a little harder now. Seeing Riley Douglas give his all could prove…rewarding.

Dear Reader,

June, the ideal month for weddings, is the perfect time to celebrate
true love. And we are doing it in style here at Silhouette Special
Edition as we celebrate the conclusion of several wonderful series.
With *For the Love of Pete*, Sherryl Woods happily marries off the
last of her ROSE COTTAGE SISTERS. It's Jo's turn this time—
and she'd thought she'd gotten Pete Catlett out of her system for
good. But at her childhood haven, anything can happen! Next,
MONTANA MAVERICKS: GOLD RUSH GROOMS concludes
with Cheryl St.John's *Million-Dollar Makeover*. We finally learn
the identity of the true heir to the Queen of Hearts Mine—and no
one is more shocked than the owner herself, the plain-Jane town...
dog walker. When she finds herself in need of financial advice,
she consults devastatingly handsome Riley Douglas—but she
soon finds his influence exceeds the business sphere....

And speaking of conclusions, Judy Duarte finishes off her
BAYSIDE BACHELORS miniseries with *The Matchmakers'*
Daddy, in which a wrongly imprisoned ex-con finds all kinds
of second chances with a beautiful single mother and her
adorable little girls. Next up in GOING HOME, Christine Flynn's
heartwarming miniseries, is *The Sugar House*, in which a man
who comes home to right a wrong finds himself falling for the
woman who's always seen him as her adversary. Patricia McLinn's
next book in her SOMETHING OLD, SOMETHING NEW...
miniseries, *Baby Blues and Wedding Bells*, tells the story of a man
who suddenly learns that his niece is really...his daughter. And in
The Secrets Between Them by Nikki Benjamin, a divorced woman
who's falling hard for her gardener learns that he is in reality an
investigator hired by her ex-father-in-law to try to prove her an unfit
mother.

So enjoy all those beautiful weddings, and be sure to come back
next month! Here's hoping you catch the bouquet....

Gail Chasan
Senior Editor

Please address questions and book requests to:
Silhouette Reader Service
U.S.: 3010 Walden Ave., P.O. Box 1325, Buffalo, NY 14269
Canadian: P.O. Box 609, Fort Erie, Ont. L2A 5X3

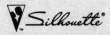

SPECIAL EDITION™

presents a new six-book continuity

MOST LIKELY TO...

Eleven students. One reunion.
And a secret that will change everyone's lives.

On sale July 2005

THE HOMECOMING HERO RETURNS

(SE #1694)

by bestselling author

Joan Elliott Pickart

Former college jock David Westport was convinced he had it all—a beautiful wife, two wonderful kids and a good business in his North End neighborhood. Sandra Westport loved her husband dearly but was positive that he did have one regret—letting her sudden pregnancy derail his chances at a pro baseball career ten years ago. And when a college professor revealed a secret that threw all the good in David's life into shadow, Sandra feared her marriage was over. Could David rebuild his shattered dreams without losing the love of his life?

Don't miss this emotional story—only from Silhouette Books.

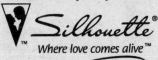

Where love comes alive™

SPECIAL EDITION™

is proud to present a dynamic new voice in romance, Jessica Bird, with the first of her Moorehouse family trilogy.

BEAUTY AND THE BLACK SHEEP

Available July 2005

The force of those eyes hit Frankie Moorehouse like a gust of wind. But she quickly reminded herself that she had dinner to get ready, a staff (such as it was) to motivate, a busines to run. She didn't have the luxury of staring into a stranger's face.

Although, jeez, what a face it was.

And wasn't it just her luck that *he* was the chef her restaurant desperately needed, and he was staying the summer....

Where love comes alive™

Next™

July 2005 from NEXT™

From the award-winning author of SAFE PASSAGE comes a compelling new novel about love, friends and sticking together.

RIGGS PARK by Ellyn Bache

www.TheNextNovel.com

Reading guide available at www.readersring.com

Four new titles available each month wherever Harlequin books are sold.

HNRP

MILLION-DOLLAR
MAKEOVER

CHERYL ST.JOHN

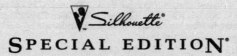

SPECIAL EDITION

Published by Silhouette Books

America's Publisher of Contemporary Romance

Special thanks and acknowledgment are given to
Cheryl St.John for her contribution to the
MONTANA MAVERICKS: GOLD RUSH GROOMS series.

 SILHOUETTE BOOKS

ISBN 0-373-24688-9

MILLION-DOLLAR MAKEOVER

CHERYL ST.JOHN

A peacemaker, a romantic, an idealist and a discouraged perfectionist are the words that Cheryl uses to describe herself. The author of both historical and contemporary novels says she's been told that she is painfully honest.

Cheryl admits to being an avid collector who collects everything from dolls to Depression glass, brass candlesticks, old photographs and—most especially—books. She and her husband love to browse antiques and collectibles shops.

She says that knowing her stories bring hope and pleasure to readers is one of the best parts of being a writer. The other wonderful part is being able to set her own schedule and have time to work around her growing family.

Cheryl loves to hear from readers. You can write her at: P.O. Box 24732, Omaha, NE 68124.

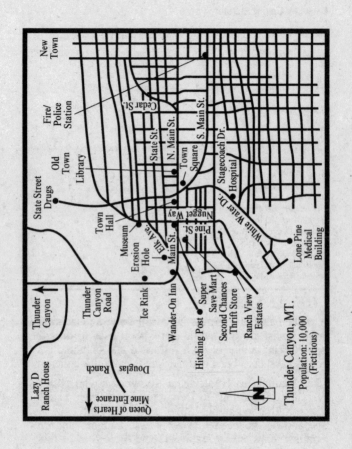

Thunder Canyon, MT.
Population: 10,000
(Fictitious)

Chapter One

"This news conference is the biggest thing that's ever happened in Thunder Canyon," the local news announcer said over the murmur of the crowd behind her.

Lisa Jane Martin glanced up from peeling the cellophane from a frozen entrée to check out the television screen. "Yeah, well, get on with it and maybe we can still see the sports and weather."

Overwhelmed by sightseers and the influx of tourists, she'd been wishing this whole gold-mine thing would blow over so Thunder Canyon would get back to the quiet norm she appreciated.

At the sound of her voice, her two golden retrievers scrambled to their feet, nails scraping against the aged wooden floor, and vied for the same space in which she stood. Joey, the brown who always looked as though he had a smile on his face, tried to wedge his way between her knees and got caught in her ankle-length skirt. "Chill, Joey."

Piper, the blonde, noticed the extra attention and squirmed closer, stepping on her foot.

"All right, all right. Sit."

Both dogs obeyed immediately. She went to a covered bin on the back porch to scoop out two bowls of dog food and placed them on the floor just inside the door.

The sound of crunching nearly obliterated the reporter's next softly spoken announcement. "The gentleman in the blue suit is the mayor's assistant. Since we've spotted him, it leads us to believe the mayor will be arriving on the scene at any moment."

Lisa poured herself a glass of milk and glanced at faces as the camera panned the crowd. A few of her pet-owner clients caught her attention. "Are people really taking this seriously? I know I had a fork out."

On the counter beside the television was a stack of mail, including a couple of registered letters she'd been ignoring, and she picked one up. "I don't think they send a letter if you've won the lottery. Do they? They phone you, probably."

That would have been a problem, too. She'd been having trouble with her antiquated answering machine for a couple of weeks and knew she'd been missing messages from clients. A new one just wasn't in the budget.

She glanced at the return address on the envelope and discovered the street number for the courthouse. Last time she'd had to sign for something, it had been a no-tification of reassessed property taxes and an adjusted fee. The real adjustment had been eating tuna for three months to make ends meet. She tossed the envelope back on the pile of mail.

The house had been a steal, so she couldn't complain. She'd inherited half upon her grandmother's death and bought the other half from her old aunt Gert's estate after the woman had passed on eight years ago.

Lisa had come to live here with her gran and her aunt Gert when she was twelve and her mother had died. Only minimal changes had been made in all those years. She kept the dark woodwork, faded wallpaper, hard-wood floors, crocheted doilies and vintage furniture well cared for. The house was her link to family and fa-miliarity, her haven and her security. It was the only place she found solitude and escape from the stigma of being the descendent of a town pariah.

"The crowd outside Town Hall waits breathlessly for the true owner of the gold mine to be announced. Over the past months, gold fever has swept the town. Here's Mayor Brookhurst now."

Portly and balding, the mayor sported a handlebar mustache that came in handy each year when he starred as the sheriff with the Olde Time Players who put on skits during the summer festival. Because of his pen-chant for melodramatic acting, Lisa had trouble taking him seriously now.

"This day will go down in Thunder Canyon's his-tory!" he predicted. "The economy of our town is about to take a turn for the better. We all knew the mine owner could be someone among us. And it is! We have a millionaire living in our midst!"

A buzz of excitement shot through the crowd gathered downtown. Lisa shook her head at the foolishness of the people who thought they were going to get rich quick.

"Humans are born into their lives and have to make of it what they will," she said to the dogs. "Nobody hands anybody a fortune on a platter."

At the ding of the microwave, she took out her dinner and seated herself at the chrome-and-red-Formica table.

"First I'd like to acknowledge and thank Brad Vaughn and Emily Stanton. These two were instrumental in the discovery of the mine's ownership. Without their investigation, we'd all still be wondering."

"Or not."

At her voice, Joey looked up and smiled.

She raised her glass of milk in a toast.

"After much researching of the Queen of Hearts claim," the mayor said, "it has been documented and proven that ownership over the years went from the original filer to Bart Divine to Lily Divine, who later became Lily Divine Harding."

The name of her infamous ancestor caught Lisa's attention. The bite she'd taken stuck in her throat and she laid down her fork. Lily Divine, Lisa's great-great-grandmother, was reputed to have been the owner of a brothel in Thunder Canyon; rumors abounded to this day.

Lisa's attention focused on what the man was saying.

The mayor held up a framed document and continued. "Lily mortgaged the deed to Amos Douglas in 1890. Proof has been uncovered that after Amos's death, his wife Catherine intended to return the deed to Lily, but the paperwork was never filed. Here's what this all boils down to, ladies and gentleman. Lily Divine was the legal owner of the claim at the time of her death."

"Wow, boys. My great-great-grandma owned a gold mine. I hope this doesn't mean people are going to ask me about it. Or about her." Unease slid into the pit of her belly at the thought of being singled out. She'd spent her whole life avoiding the rumors and the stigma surrounding the legend.

The camera zoomed in for a close-up of the mayor, and a hush fell over the crowd. "Today we know that the rightful owner of the Queen of Hearts gold mine is... *Lisa Jane Martin,* a lifetime resident of Thunder Canyon and the only living descendent of Lily Divine Harding."

The last bite Lisa'd taken swelled to the size of a grapefruit behind her breastbone and wouldn't come up or go down. She choked and tried to breathe, to swallow, to do anything but strangle. She stumbled to the chipped porcelain sink and ran a glass of water. She must have heard wrong!

After two glasses of water, the bite went down. She grabbed a paper towel and wiped her chin. When her eyes stopped watering, she turned back to the TV.

Reporters were vying to ask questions and *her* name kept being mentioned! It was definitely her name. She stared and turned up the volume just in case her hearing had been affected by her near choking death.

"So far Miss Martin hasn't responded to our attempts to reach her."

Her gaze shot to the registered letters. *Oh, crap.*

"But we've learned her address and she will be contacted immediately."

"Oh, no." She was going to throw up. There was nothing worse than attention. Nothing. Lisa went *out of her way* to go unnoticed. She'd always been an introvert. Always.

She'd have to escape before they found her. She yanked her denim jacket from the back of the kitchen chair and shrugged into it, fighting with the collar that stubbornly turned under.

Grabbing one of her four key rings, she stared at the keys to dozens of homes. Homes with pets counting on her for their daily walk or for their food and care while their owners were away. She couldn't run out on her animals. They'd be unattended and no one would know.

There were three dogs in her fenced-in backyard right now, pets in her care during their owners' trips. She couldn't just leave, and she had no one to take over for her. She wandered blindly toward the front of the house wondering how she could avoid this. She'd had to live down Lily Divine's reputation her whole life. Gran and Aunt Gert had been sympathetic and accepting, but they were her father's family, not her mother's. They hadn't shared the black mark of a hussy forebear.

Reeling with confusion, Lisa paused in the hall and leaned back against the papered wall.

Piper came to comfort her first, and she bent forward to receive his devoted concern. Joey followed, finding her ear and giving it a swipe with his tongue.

She had just dried her ear on her sleeve when the doorbell rang.

Her gaze jerked upward.

The dogs barked.

Without thinking, she headed for the entrance. Both dogs ran ahead of her, and she tripped over Piper, catching the doorknob to steady herself. Instinctively she opened the door.

People. A lot of them. Flashes went off, blinding her. A dozen cameras whirred, and boom mikes swung over the heads of the reporters who crowded her front porch. She realized her mistake too late. Barking frantically at all the strangers, her dogs darted out into the throng.

"Have you been following the story of the Queen of Hearts?"

"What are you going to do with the money?"

"Miss Martin, look this way. Are you planning to mine right away?"

"Over here, Miss Martin! What's your favorite charity?"

"What about environmental protection?"

Frazzled, Lisa tried to see over and around the inquiring reporters in hopes of spotting her dogs. Even if she had an answer, she wouldn't have spoken in public—and definitely not before a television camera.

"Piper! Come!" She pushed her way through the crush and down the porch stairs. "Joey! Heel!"

"Miss Martin, just a few questions, please."

She spotted traitorous Joey making friends with a blond woman in a black pantsuit with pink trim. His tail wagged and he was smiling at her. Lisa made a lunge and grabbed his collar. "Heel."

Piper, obviously the smarter of the two, had a photographer backed up against the trunk of her oak tree and was growling menacingly. She'd never seen him bite anyone, but this fellow would have made a good start, judging from the camera on his shoulder.

After seizing Piper, she dragged both dogs back to the house, across the porch, then slammed and locked the door in the wake of the television and newspaper personnel.

"I hope you boys did your business out there just now, 'cause we're not opening that door again."

The doorbell rang and she covered her ears at the shrill barks that followed. "Get off my property! I'm calling the police!" she shouted through the door.

The doorbell didn't ring again, but the porch floor creaked, and an occasional peek through the lace curtains revealed that several curious information seekers still waited out front to catch her. Eventually she would have to let the dogs out the back. Eventually she would have to feed her clients' dogs. Sooner or later she'd have to go for groceries or starve. The stomach ache that had come on wasn't from hunger, though. It was a sick vulnerability that ached all the way through to her innards.

The phone rang.

For a minute she just listened to the persistent jangle. She'd had so much trouble retrieving messages, she'd gotten fed up with the hassle and had turned off the machine. The phone continued to ring.

If she had caller ID, she'd know whether it was a pet owner or a reporter, she thought belatedly. Until this moment she'd always thought paying to know who was calling—when you could just pick up the phone and see—was a ridiculous expense.

Lisa walked to the kitchen and picked up the receiver on a bright yellow dial wall phone. "Hello?"

"Miss Martin," the male voice said. "This is Mayor Brookhurst's assistant. Congratulations! The mayor would like to invite you to Town Hall so we can present you with the deed to the Queen of Hearts and get a couple of signatures. Just official red-tape stuff but necessary. We thought this would be a good time because the local newspeople are still on the scene."

"I'm not walking out my door."

"Excuse me?"

"I don't know how there could be any reporters left there, because they've overrun my yard and my porch and are trampling my petunias."

"It's a lot of excitement, isn't it? Thunder Canyon's never had so many tourists. I'm told we'll be on the national news this evening."

"I don't want to be a news story—national, local or late breaking. Nothing. And I want these guys out of my yard."

"But, Miss Martin, this is a huge story. You've just inherited a gold mine."

"I don't want it."

"But— But—" He sputtered for a moment. "I'm sorry, but it's yours."

She hung up.

Another peek revealed cars and news-station vans parked along the tree-lined street and people milling in her front yard, the shadows of the boldest haunting her front porch.

The backyard entered her thoughts, and she bolted through the house to look out the window in the rear door. A few casually dressed men walked the perimeter of the six-foot chain-link fence, from inside of which the collie and the sheltie barked. The dachshund wagged his tail and ran in circles.

Lisa ordered her dogs to stay while she opened the door and called to the others. "Brigette! Monty! Aggie! Come in!" She made kissing noises, and the three dogs darted inside. She promptly shut the door and locked it. She wasn't about to open a door again without a good reason.

The visiting pets found the food she'd put out for Joey and Piper, and a growling match ensued until she got out more bowls. The crunching intensified. *Oh, dear. Poop.* Poop was a good reason to open the door, but she wouldn't think about that until the time came.

Her phone rang again. She considered taking it off the hook, but something drove her to pick it up and listen.

"Lisa? Lisa, this is Emily Stanton. I've been involved in the case of finding the owner of the mine."

Lisa remembered seeing the woman introduced on the news.

"I'm right outside your front door. I promise to respect your privacy. I'd like to do whatever I can to help you. We need to talk, and there are some legal matters that need your attention. Can we talk? Please?"

"I'm not talking to any reporters."

"I'm not asking you to. I'm asking for a few minutes of your time to go over this situation. Just the two of us."

Lisa didn't say anything.

"Tell you what—I'll call the mayor right now. He'll contact the sheriff and have the newspeople removed. Does that show my good faith?"

"You could do that?"

"I'll do it right now."

Ten minutes later Lisa saw half a dozen sheriff's vehicles pull up alongside the other cars on the street. Officers spoke to reporters and ushered them away from Lisa's yard.

Lisa craned to see the woman standing near the front door. She moved to the foyer and called, "Emily?"

"I'm still here."

Lisa opened the door six inches to peer out. A young woman with straight, shoulder-length brown hair and green eyes gazed back at her. Lisa opened the door and Emily slipped in as a camera whirred.

Lisa closed the door and locked it.

Five dogs surrounded Emily, and her eyebrows rose in surprise. "Oh, my. You're a dog lover."

"Yes. But they're not all mine. I pet sit."

"I think I heard that somewhere. Your business is called Puppy Love?"

She nodded. "It seemed like I was always taking care of someone's pet when I was in high school. It just sort of turned into my livelihood."

"So, you bring pets home with you?"

"Only by special arrangement. Normally I go to their homes. I walk dogs during the day when their owners are at work, or I go a couple times a day when people are on vacation."

They glanced at each other in the awkward way people who don't know each other do.

"I work for Vaughn Associates," Emily said. "At least, I did until just a little while ago when my boss proposed to me on television."

"I must have been choking during that part. Congratulations."

"Thank you. Anyway, we're a private investigation firm hired to track the gold-mine heir." She gestured toward Lisa as she corrected, "Or heiress."

Lisa gave her a weak smile. "I don't want a gold mine."

Lisa noticed Emily's glance at the hallway slide to the living room. So what if her house looked as though it had been furnished and decorated fifty years ago? It had. She liked it this way.

"No, really, I like my house and everything just the way it is."

"We're talking a lot of money here," Emily said. "I don't want to tell you what to do, but…lives could change. We're talking about the economy of Thunder Canyon. About not only how your life can be enriched but what you could do with the profits. Think about it, Lisa. Haven't you thought of things you would do if you had money? I have. I'd be able to pay for my younger sister to finish college. And I've always thought I'd start a scholarship for young women. Isn't there something you've always dreamed you could do if you had the resources?"

Lisa shrugged. "The humane societies are underfunded and understaffed. I'd build an animal shelter. A no-kill facility where pets could live if no one adopted them."

Emily smiled. "You can do that now."

"Are you sure this is all...legal? This is for real?"

"It's for real. You own the Queen of Hearts. Caleb Douglas's experts have assessed a substantial vein. Because of all the gold diggers swarming the area, the Douglases arranged security some time ago. You'll be responsible for taking that over and making arrangements for how you want to proceed with the mining."

Just the thought made Lisa feel panicked. "I don't know anything about mining."

"There are people to help you. I suggest you hire a lawyer first thing. Someone with your best interests at heart, someone you trust. Then a financial manager."

Lisa passed a shaking hand over her eyes. "It's too much to think about."

Emily leaned over the back of the sofa to peer out between the lace curtains on the window. "The only car left out front on this side is my rental. The mayor has ordered the press to stay off your property and on the other side of the street. I'll take you to Town Hall, and you can file a restraining order against the press. Then I'll stay with you while you sign the deed papers. Okay?"

Lisa didn't know that she had much choice. People were not going to leave her alone until this was taken care of and the news blew over. "I'll put the dogs in their kennels."

Emily nodded.

The afternoon passed in a blur of meetings and legal talk. Lisa was placed in touch with the Montana Mining Association, several environmental agencies, The Office of Historical Preservation and the Bureau of Land Management. The operational and engineering issues would have to be decided, and she hadn't a clue what to do. Head spinning, Lisa just wished she could evade all the publicity and trouble.

She took Emily's advice and hired a lawyer. A woman Emily recommended. Bernadine Albright was more than willing to clear her afternoon schedule to meet with Lisa. Holding the press at bay, Emily drove Lisa to the lawyer's office.

Complete strangers were excited and animated, congratulating her and bringing her soft drinks and cups of coffee. The inheritance and the experience seemed unreal. Complicated. Overwhelming. She didn't want her life to change.

Lisa had too much to absorb and think about, and this was all happening too fast. More than anything else she feared was the fact that her life was never going to be the same.

Riley Douglas handed a stack of papers to the secretary who'd just arrived at their downtown building for the day and strode down the hall to his father's office.

At sixty-six, Caleb still had a thick head of silver hair and a physique toned from keeping a hand in the working operation of his ranch. He'd kept his recent bouts with heart disease a secret from their colleagues and the community, and Riley was one of the few to recognize fatigue and stress taking a toll on the man. Right now Caleb's face was red with anger. Riley picked up the phone and punched in a number. "I'm calling Dr. Simms. You're not supposed to be getting riled up like this."

Focused on this latest ghastly situation, Caleb waved

Riley's comment away. The enormous black-lacquer armoire was open, the television tuned to the local news yet again. On Caleb's desk was last evening's paper as well as today's special morning edition, both displaying the pages which relayed the gold-mine story.

"We've got to do something," Caleb insisted. "That's been Douglas land for four generations. No bohemian dogsitter is going to take it away from us."

Waiting to speak with the doctor, Riley watched footage of the young woman for the hundredth time. First they showed her chasing two dogs out her front door. Dressed in a long skirt, tennis shoes and a denim jacket, she was a fashion casualty if he'd ever seen one. Her dark hair could use an extreme makeover, as well, parted on one side and sprouting wild ringlets that fell to her shoulders.

She stared at the camera as though she'd been caught committing a crime, then jerked into motion, calling her dogs. She tripped over the huge beasts, tripped over the hem of her wallpaper-print skirt, then retreated back into her house and slammed the door.

"Doc, can you spare a call to my father's downtown office? I'll never get him to yours. He's taking his blood-pressure medicine, but I don't like the way he looks. Thanks." Riley hung up and kept watching.

The next video clip was taken as Lisa Martin and Emily Stanton approached Town Hall. With swinging dark hair, Emily was cool and professional, guiding the dowdy heiress through the crowd of reporters on the street and into the building, with the assistance of half a dozen police officers. This little town had never seen so many law-enforcement officials. The state patrol and the sheriff's department had been on call since early reports of the gold strike had been leaked months ago.

The following shot was of Lisa Jane Martin riding in the passenger side of a silver Chrysler Intrepid as Emily pulled away followed by a camera crew. They'd shown these same clips over and over since the night before. Reporters had used every rags-to-riches phrase they could come up with and had dubbed the Martin girl Cinderella.

And then came the picture someone had culled from a past Thunder Canyon High yearbook, a photograph of a dark-haired girl who looked vaguely familiar. According to the caption under the likeness, she'd graduated two years behind him, so it was possible he'd seen her in the halls. Nothing remarkable about her. Nothing that would have garnered more than a passing glance.

She was either divorced or never married, he guessed, since her name was still Martin and she lived in the house where she'd lived with relatives since her mother's death. After one day of news, he knew more about Lisa Jane Martin than he did about the women he dated.

"She's single," he said thoughtfully.

His father finally removed his gaze from the television. His eyebrows rose and a glimmer of hope sparkled in his eyes. "Yes. Yes, she is."

Chapter Two

Lisa opened her eyes and stared at the plaster ceiling. Saw the same two cracks that had been there the day before and the week before that and the month before that. She sat up, and beside her both retrievers woke and yawned. Joey placed his front feet on the floor first, stretching with his hind feet on the bed, then slowly stepped down. Piper bounded from the bed in one leap and danced in front of her while she stumbled to the bathroom. "Hold on a sec."

A few minutes later, she peered out the curtained window of the back door, let the three dogs out of the utility room and loosed all five into the backyard. The click of a shutter reached her through the morning stillness. She couldn't see anyone, but sun momentarily glinted off a distant object. There was a wooded area behind her house, and it *was* possible someone could wait out there with a telephoto lens. "Get a life!" she shouted and shut the door.

While she made coffee and poured orange juice, she watched the dogs through the window over the sink. They seemed unconcerned with anything other than their morning sniff-and-pee routine, so she guessed all was clear.

She turned on the television, looking for her morning show and instead saw her own image plastered across the screen. She raised one hand to her hair in horror.

"Oh, my. Oh, my." The Lisa on the screen looked as if she'd been struck by lightning coming out of the Salvation Army store. Her goal had always been anonymity, but her appearance called attention by its very weirdness.

The clips of her with Emily emphasized her drab fluffiness next to Emily's clean lines.

What could be so interesting that all those feet of film were being taken of *her?* A million dollars, she gleaned from the commentary and shook her head. She still had no concept of her inheritance.

The next image induced a groan. She'd always detested that high school picture. While other girls' parents had forked over an arm and a leg for touched-up studio work, she'd found the very least expensive photographer in the area. She'd never thought it would make a difference. Who would see it after all?

Lisa flipped channels. The very same picture was plastered on CNN footage. *Only a few million people had seen it.*

Mind reeling, she turned off the TV. The real problem was how she was going to take care of her pets today without being followed. She had filled out paperwork for a restraining order and the judge had signed it. The press was required to stay a hundred feet away from her and out of her yard. She had twelve homes to visit this morning, then meetings with the security people and the mining association in the afternoon.

She let the dogs in and they ate while she fixed herself breakfast. She slipped on her neon-green garden boots and washed out the kennels and runs, filled bowls with water, then locked the dogs into the shaded runs for the day.

After showering, she considered her wardrobe. Whatever she donned, it would be on the news tonight. A pretty mind-boggling concept. There wasn't much choice. Only long skirts hung in her closet, so she chose one and dressed, found a white ball cap to hide her hair and donned a pair of sunglasses.

Her rusty old green Blazer started with a puff of smoke, but it started, and she pulled out of her drive. A glance in the rearview mirror showed three SUVs with satellite dishes following her.

She'd seen clips of Madonna, J.Lo and Gwyneth Paltrow being hounded by reporters, and she'd wondered how they ever managed to go anywhere in private. That she was facing the same problem today was surreal.

Having an audience took the joy from a task she usually enjoyed. Caring for her pets, walking the dogs and knowing they were getting attention, was normally rewarding. Today she felt as if she were under a microscope. And she was. She took three dogs at a time in her Blazer, walking them on leashes through the park and politely picking up after them with plastic bags, which she disposed of in trash barrels.

"Heiress picks up collie poop," she said to herself. "Film at eleven." Jake, the collie in question, barked at the cameraman across the street. The dog's owner drove to a nearby town to work and paid Lisa to walk the animal once a day during his absence. Lisa scratched Jake's ears. "Unnerving, isn't it, to do your business with paparazzi watching? Maybe a talent scout will discover you and you'll be the next fast-food icon. You like tacos?"

Dogs eventually walked and cats all fed, Lisa drove home to grab a quick lunch. A new white Expedition pulled into her drive behind her, and a forty-something woman got out. "I saw Aggie on CNN last night! You, too, of course."

Lisa nodded. "Smile. You'll probably see yourself tonight."

Barbara Cooper, owner of the dachshund in Lisa's backyard, glanced around and fluffed her hair with her fingers. "Are you serious?"

"'Fraid so. Did you have a good trip?"

Barbara tugged the front of her shirt neatly into place and followed Lisa into the house. "It was work, what can I say? Did Aggie behave herself?"

"A sweetheart, as always."

When they reached the kitchen, Barbara took a check from her purse and handed it to Lisa. She was one of Lisa's longtime clients, though they'd never had a personal conversation until now. "So you own the gold mine?"

Lisa nodded. "That's what they tell me. It's official, because I signed all the paperwork yesterday. It's still not real, though."

"What are you going to do?" Barbara asked as they walked out to the backyard.

After handing the woman Aggie's retractable leash, Lisa opened the kennel door and the dachshund shot out. "What do you mean?"

Barbara knelt and scooped up her pet. "Surely you won't be taking in dogs anymore. I don't know where I'll find someone else I trust who really cares for Aggie the way you do."

Lisa petted Aggie's head. "I can't imagine not taking in my dogs," she replied. "They're like friends who come to see me."

Barbara fastened the leash on the dog's collar and set her pet down. "We'll see. Somehow I don't think you'll be interested next time. You'll be busy."

"Doing what?"

"Spending money. And I won't blame you. That's what I'd be doing." She walked toward the side gate. "Well, congratulations. And thanks."

Lisa watched her go, checked the water dishes and fixed herself a peanut-butter-and-potato-chip sandwich.

When she walked out her front door, a dark blue limo waited at the curb. The driver, who'd been standing beside the rear door, tipped his hat. "Miss Martin."

She took several steps forward. Mayor Brookhurst had told her he'd work out the details of her meetings. "This is for me?"

He nodded. "Yes, miss. Mr. Douglas sent me for you."

Everyone in Thunder Canyon knew of Caleb Douglas. Even Lisa, who shied away from people and the places they gathered, had heard the talk. Occasionally Lisa cared for Adele's enormous poodle, but she'd never run into Caleb during any of her visits.

Gran had never had much use for the man or his high-handed wife, but because of their wealth and property holdings, none could deny the Douglases were pillars of the community.

"You're taking me to the security meeting?"

"Yes, miss."

There had been talk recently about how the Douglases had come to claim ownership of the Queen of Hearts mine. She'd learned from Emily that the Douglases had hired her firm to prove their legal claim, but that the investigation had proven otherwise.

Whether she liked it or not, Lisa was up to her neck in this gold-mine business. She was going to have to be better informed, she concluded, slipping inside the limo and seating herself on the soft leather as the driver closed the door. She had a lot more questions for Emily.

She surveyed the elegant interior and marveled at over half a dozen sparkling glasses set into wells on a minibar. Absently she wondered what was a good peanut-butter chaser. Noticing then that the driver was smoothly driving out of Thunder Canyon, Lisa experienced a touch of apprehension. She tapped on the Plexiglas divider. It rolled down silently and the driver asked, "Yes, Miss Martin?"

"Where are we going?"

"To Mr. Douglas's office at the Lazy D."

"Oh. Okay."

The countryside was beautiful, so she enjoyed the scenery. Horses grazed behind miles of white fence, and seed-tipped hay fields waved in the sunlight. Finally they passed through a gate proclaiming the Lazy D ranch. Since Lisa looked after Adele's dog while the couple vacationed, she was familiar with the grandeur of the home. Instead of heading for the circular drive where the main home, guesthouse, foreman's cottage and bunkhouse sat, however, the driver took a road that wound away. Did Caleb have offices elsewhere?

After another half mile, she was getting ready to tap on the Plexiglas again when the driver pulled to a stop before a sprawling stone house and got out to assist her.

"Go on in, miss. Mr. Douglas is expecting you."

Lisa hesitantly climbed the stairs and opened the door. She entered into a huge foyer. Shiny wood floors reflected a massive hall table beneath a chandelier. Definitely not the same stuffy decor as the other place. "Hello?"

"Miss Martin."

She turned, expecting the silver-haired man she'd seen on the news. Instead a younger man, tall with black hair and intense green eyes, greeted her. Her immediate reaction was that she should turn and run right back out the door, but her feet were rooted to the spot. He wore a sport jacket, white shirt, jeans and boots. Casual attire, but on this man they made her feel even more inappropriately dressed. She'd have taken off her ball cap, but her hair was matted to her head by now.

She did slip off the sunglasses and drop them into her denim handbag. She felt exposed in his presence…vulnerable. And she didn't like it.

He strode forward and extended a hand. "Riley Douglas."

In the flesh. He was taller and leaner than she remembered from school, his features sharpened to devastating virility by the past ten years. He looked even better than he had then. "I know—I mean, yes."

She took his strong, warm hand for an instant, and then he released hers.

"I was expecting…your father."

"He'll be along. I handled all the security for the mine, so I thought I should bring you up to speed and answer any questions. He does want to meet you later, though. Come on back to my office. I asked you here early so we could get acquainted and go over a few things. Once the security team arrives, there won't be much chance for us to talk privately."

Lisa followed him down a hall bordered on one side by floor-to-ceiling windows that let in the sun and offered a stunning view of the ranch.

She'd been expecting dark wood, but his office was all black leather, chrome and glass. On a counter in one corner, two coffeepots were just finishing perking, but he gestured to the wet bar. "Care for a drink?"

This was a good-old-boy operation, she surmised, and probably a good many deals were negotiated over drinks. If his associates drank in the limo, as well, how did anyone make it through meetings sober?

"No, thanks."

"The wine's been breathing for about fifteen minutes," he said.

Lisa glanced at the bottle sitting in a bucket of ice.

Several others stood at the ready on the bar nearby. She did enjoy a glass of wine now and then, and the labels on those bottles indicated he hadn't picked them up at the same grocery store where she shopped. And he'd already opened one, she rationalized.

"Sure. Thanks."

He picked up the bottle and poured a stemmed glass three-quarters full.

She accepted the wine with a twinge of regret, because she knew she wouldn't drink a whole bottle, and it looked expensive.

"Does it suit you?"

"What? Oh." She tasted the white wine. It was better than anything she'd ever tried. "It's excellent."

He poured himself a tonic water and gestured for her to sit on one of the black leather sofas. She did, and he sat across from her.

"I'm glad we have this chance to meet."

No surprise that he didn't remember her. Having skipped fifth grade, Lisa had been a young freshman. She'd noticed Riley Douglas right away and secretly admired his good looks and popularity. She'd been his assigned tutor for chemistry, and spending two evenings a week together had afforded more than enough opportunity for her to develop a full-blown crush. He'd always been polite and friendly enough, though distant. She hadn't been his type then any more than she was now, and he'd easily dismissed their relationship after he'd passed his class.

It had been okay then. It was okay now. "Yes," was all she said.

"Would you like to go over the arrangements I had worked out with the security people? You might prefer to hire a company of your own choice, but we've used Weber Security exclusively for the last eight years. I can recommend them highly."

"Exactly what needs to be protected? I don't have any idea."

"Do you remember how this whole gold-mine thing came about?"

"Vaguely."

"In February the son of the high school coach disappeared."

"I remember that. The Stevenson boy was found in the mine shaft and rescued."

Riley nodded. "And a rescue worker found a gold nugget. That started the gold fever. On more than one occasion after that vandals broke into the cordoned-off mine site."

"I saw news reports that some of them were injured. The clinic was hopping."

"Things got pretty crazy. Anyway, that property had been counted as part of Douglas holdings for generations, but suddenly our ownership was questioned. Believing our claim would be verified, we secured the area. We've had a perimeter guard and armed security at the site round-the-clock since mid-February, in part to protect what we thought was our property as well as to prevent any more mining injuries."

Security guards. Oh, my.

"Now that the investigators have proven the land belonged to Lily Divine—and, in that case, to *me*—all along, will you want to be reimbursed for those costs?" Lisa was beginning to question the wisdom of coming here, of talking to a Douglas without her lawyer. "I think I should call my lawyer. May I use your phone?"

"Of course." He gestured to the desktop. "I assure you I wasn't thinking of reimbursement."

"It would seem only right," she insisted.

"It's petty, Miss Martin, and I won't entertain further discussion in the matter."

She raised her eyebrows. "Excuse me." She punched numbers, and Bernadine Albright took her call immediately.

"You were wise to call me, Lisa. I'll be right there. Don't agree to anything until then."

Lisa hung up the phone. "She's on her way."

Riley raised his glass. "Good decision. Until she arrives, we'll get to know each other a little better."

Lisa didn't want the wine to go to waste, so she accepted another glass. She glanced out the double glass doors that opened onto a brick patio. In the distance she saw a modern red barn. "Is this where you live?"

"And work. Built the house a few years ago."

"You run the ranch?"

"I help. My father is the hands-on rancher. I'm the financial manager. Over the past couple years I've devoted myself to expanding our real-estate ventures."

She remembered reading about him going off to college and later coming home with a degree in finance. Lisa walked to the doors and looked out over the pastureland where several horses grazed.

"Do you ride?" he asked from directly behind her.

Goose bumps rose on her shoulders and arms at his nearness. "I used to ride when Mr. McKinley had his stables north of town."

"Poor old nags." Riley chuckled. "They were long in the tooth and not much for looking at."

"Not everyone has his own breeding stock in the backyard," she replied.

He shrugged off her comment. "Maybe you'd like to come out and ride sometime. Anytime. Consider it an open invitation."

Riley Douglas was only one of the many people who'd suddenly found it in their hearts to befriend her. Funny how people who hadn't given her the time of day a week ago were now pursuing her attention.

She definitely questioned this man's sincerity. She may have inherited a gold mine, but she hadn't gotten any better looking.

She moved back into the room and studied the pieces of artwork. Modern paintings and a few sculptures. No photographs. She couldn't recall hearing mention of Riley ever marrying. Sometimes local gossip had him paired with one particular woman or another, all of them out of her league. Why his marital status should matter was questionable, but she sure was wondering.

"Did you do your own decorating in here?"

He nodded. "Is it that obvious? Pretty hit-and-miss, actually. I just pick up things I like when I'm traveling."

The place seemed a little sparse and modern for her taste, but what did she know? She hadn't spent money on more than a plug-in air freshener for her house in the last five years. And the only stuff she picked up while traveling was dog poop.

There was a knock at a side door, and it opened without Riley's consent. A thin woman wearing a dark green pantsuit carried a tray of small sandwiches into the room and placed it on the low glass coffee table. Lisa caught herself imagining setting anything edible on a table this low in her house.

The woman turned to the counter area, where she disposed of coffee grounds and set out several glossy black mugs, each one with a fancy *D* on the side.

"Do you need anything else, Mr. Douglas?"

"This looks great, Marge, thank you."

After she'd gone, Riley gestured to the food. "Help yourself."

Lisa perched on the leather sofa and looked over the selection with interest. Riley politely waited until she made a decision, then seated himself and picked up a napkin and a couple of sandwiches.

The thick chicken salad had chunks of walnuts and sliced grapes, and Lisa wondered how many she could consume without looking like an oinker. They sure beat her peanut-butter-and-potato-chip special.

Riley refilled her glass, and she felt a lot more comfortable here than she had at first. If he was trying to soften her up for something with food and wine, it was working. It was a good thing she'd called Bernadine. She was going to need a designated driver.

Her lawyer showed up a few minutes later. When Riley poured the woman a glass of brandy and offered her a sandwich, she met Lisa's gaze with a knowing look. But she ate and drank as their discussion got under way.

Riley showed them the contract he had with Weber Security and explained the situation. "Weber is willing to switch the contract over to your company without a hitch. Have you incorporated?"

"Lisa and I are working on that today," Bernadine said.

"This is all happening so fast," Lisa told him. "There's so much to do and to understand."

"Hiring Ms. Albright was wise," Riley told her. "And having her present when you make decisions is to your benefit. But in addition I believe you're going to need a financial manager."

Emily had told her the same thing.

"*And* an advisor," he added. "Someone to help you with investments. Someone who knows the markets and can help you manage and save money."

Lisa glanced at Bernadine, who nodded. "He's right. I can look over the legal stuff, but money management and investment are out of my field."

"Is there someone like that around here?" Lisa asked.

"A manager and an advisor are two different jobs." Riley eased back comfortably on the sofa. "I'm a manager, and I'd be the best man to work with."

"But isn't that a conflict of interest?"

"How so? You pay me for my services and I make money off your money. I'd be doing the best I knew how, just like I do for my own holdings and my father's."

"Do you have the time? Surely you have a lot on your plate right now. I've read about the ski-resort project. That has to be a huge responsibility."

"Thinking the mine was a Douglas property, I had already cleared time to handle it. This way I'd still be involved, but in your employ."

Those words perked her interest more than all the others. "You'd work for me?"

"More or less. Yes."

The concept was just too delicious. Riley Douglas, son of one of the richest families in Montana, working for the town dog walker, the great-great-granddaughter of Thunder Canyon's infamous Lily Divine. Lisa wanted to giggle. She held her exuberance inside with considerable fortitude, so it came out as more of a hiccup.

Bernadine glanced at her.

"Excuse me." She hid her smile behind a cocktail napkin.

"Think about it for a day or so," Riley suggested. "We'll talk again. How's that?"

"Unbelievable," she replied.

"What's that?"

"It's doable," she answered. "But you said it was two jobs. What about the investment part?"

"I work with someone who's always on top of things. You could either hire him or ask him to recommend someone. Phil Wagner has advised my father and I for several years, and I can hook you up. He's a savvy market man."

Riley did seem to have the know-how and the contacts she needed. His willingness to participate was flattering but a little unnerving.

Caleb arrived next, dressed in a western-cut sport jacket and a beige Stetson. He hung the hat on a rack inside the door and joined them.

"Dad, this is Bernadine Albright."

"We've met," Bernadine said, and extended a hand. Caleb leaned forward to greet her.

"And you're Lisa Jane Martin," Caleb said before Riley could introduce her. He took in her appearance with keen interest. "I guess the cap is your disguise?"

"It must not be working. You knew who I was."

"I've seen you on television. Is my son being a good host?"

"As hosts go, he ranks right up there with the best I've known." No man had offered her heavenly chicken sandwiches or plied her with wine before, so Riley was the best so far.

The security team arrived then. Lisa was disappointed that the rest of the time would be devoted to actual business, but the hard edges of Weber Security's facts and figures were softly rounded by the incredible buzz she'd acquired.

Craig Murphy headed the organization and had a manner of making people feel that he was in charge and that things were taken care of. Lisa liked and trusted him immediately. He showed her the initial police reports, maps detailing the whereabouts of his people at all times and a list of the men working the mine and explained the success of their plan thus far.

"These are the arrangements you made with Mr. Douglas?" she asked.

"Yes," he concurred. "And if this strategy works for you, we'll continue without change or interruption and simply switch the contracts over to you."

"We're not sure exactly how that's going to work

yet," Bernadine told him and explained their need to incorporate. "There are a lot of things still being worked out."

"Tell you what," Riley said. "Let's leave it the way it is for the time being. I'll pick up the tab. As soon as Miss Martin has her corporation set up and some money in her accounts, we'll do the new paperwork then."

"And reimburse you then?" Lisa asked.

"Only for services from this date forward," he answered.

"We'll need a simple agreement in writing," Bernadine added.

"Fine by me," Craig said.

Lisa and Bernadine concurred and accepted Riley's offer.

The meeting ended, and Lisa was one of the last to walk out of his office behind Bernadine. Riley and his father accompanied them.

"I'm glad we had this opportunity to meet," Caleb said.

"Likewise." She pulled out her sunglasses and slipped them on. "We meet with the Montana Mining Association this afternoon."

"Feel free to call me anytime if you need an opinion or advice," Riley told her. He gestured to the limousine at the curb. "Your ride."

"I'm riding with Bernadine from here, thanks."

She got into the lawyer's crème-colored New Yorker and glanced out the window at the two men who watched the car pull away.

"What kind of feeling did you get?" Bernadine asked.

Her feelings for Riley Douglas had been adolescent yearnings she'd outgrown years ago. "Why? What did you see?"

"Well, with Caleb I'm not sure that what you see is what you get, and I suspect the apple doesn't fall far from the tree."

"You don't trust Riley to manage us?"

"That's the odd thing. He's a hell of a financier, and we'd be missing out on using his genius brain for handling money if we didn't hook up with him. I *would* trust him as your manager. He knows what he's doing. But he probably has an ulterior motive, and we'd better have our loins girded for whatever that may be."

"What might his motive be?"

Bernadette cocked a brow at her. "Hello?"

"Money."

The woman merely nodded as she drove.

"Forewarned is girded, right? We let him do his money thing, and we watch for anything fishy."

"Watching is good," Bernadine replied.

Lisa thought about all the times she'd watched Riley Douglas. Watched him frown as he struggled with chemistry homework; watched him stroll the halls with that distinctive swagger; watched him on the football field as cheerleaders swamped him. Watching Riley was no hardship.

The interesting thing this time was that he was actually paying attention to her, knew her name, had sought her out. She didn't have any illusions that his interest was in anything other than the glittering gold mine she'd inherited, but the attention was, to say the least, flattering.

She might as well enjoy her new status. Who knew what would come of it?

Chapter Three

So much for the ball cap and the sunglasses. Lisa sat cross-legged on her sofa, her Lean Cuisine Mexican dinner in her lap, and stared at the television. Tonight's recap showed her hosing out the dog runs with untamed morning hair, wearing a pink tank top with yellow polka-dot pajama bottoms and the neon-green rubber boots.

"You people suck!" She sat her dinner on the coffee table and got up to stomp across the room to the front door. She turned the bolt lock and flung open the door. "You suck! Don't you have anything better to do?"

Her neighbor, Mrs. Carlson, had been setting her sprinkler to water her rose bushes, and she straightened to stare at Lisa. She always stared at Lisa, always seemed to be censoring her every coming and going, so the stare was nothing new.

"Oh, hey, Mrs. Carlson."

Piper tried to wedge past Lisa's legs, so she closed the door to keep him in and went back to resume her place. The last image on the screen was the high school picture again, just before the news moved on to footage of a water-main break downtown. Thank God there were a few disasters to occasionally take the focus away from her.

Joey burped from beside the sofa.

Lisa lowered her gaze to the empty tray where her burritos and rice had been. The tray had barely been moved, but it looked as clean as any of the dishes in her cupboards.

She met the dog's gaze and he smiled.

"Real funny. Now I get to eat peanut butter again. That was the last dinner, and I don't want to go to the store."

She ransacked the cupboards and finally ate a handful of trail mix and poured out the expired milk.

"Okay, tomorrow I'll go to the store."

Piper laid his head on her lap when she sat at the kitchen table and opened the phone book.

"I'll get you a chewy, but none for Joey."

At his name, the retriever padded into the room and stood watching her with expectation.

"Don't complain to me about heartburn, you pig." She got up, dialed the phone on the wall and ordered a pizza.

"Lisa Martin?" the voice on the other end of the line said. "Awesome! I just saw you on TV."

"Yeah."

"That's really cool, you owning the mine and all."

"Yeah, cool."

"We'll get your pizza there right away. You want any bread sticks or a two-liter or anything?"

She remembered a couple cans of beer in the back of her fridge. "No, thanks."

An hour later, she'd eaten her fill of her pan-fried-crust pepperoni pizza, finished a beer and was watching one of her favorite romantic movies. A comfort night she'd needed badly.

Here in her private haven, she was in her zone. The dogs had edged their way onto the sofa on either side of her, and she stroked their ears and heads.

As the movie drew to an end, she blinked back tears and drew a deep breath. "Oh, my—Joey, you *dog!*"

Now her tears weren't brought on by sentiment but by the Mexican dinner the canine had consumed.

She herded both dogs to the back door and stepped out for fresh air. "You're not sleeping with me if you keep that up."

Her boys ran along the fence and sniffed. Piper growled deep in his throat. Lisa glanced at the dark sky and the woods behind the house, not liking the constant feeling of being observed. "Suppose they have infrared, too?" She waved for good measure. "Let's go back in, boys."

Their tags jingled as they joined her.

The Super Saver Mart opened at seven the next morning, and Lisa was in the parking lot waiting for the doors to be unlocked. The television vans were parked at the farthest sides of the lot.

A newer car pulled up to a front slot, and the driver glanced toward the building. Just a customer, Lisa assured herself.

She'd showered and fixed her hair before cleaning the runs that morning and she'd found a skirt that looked less like wallpaper than all the rest. Her denim jacket fit nicely, but her tennis shoes were simply the most comfortable for grocery shopping.

After glancing at her reflection in the rearview mirror and knowing her hair was hopeless, she caught sight of someone unlocking the doors from inside the store and got out of her Blazer. She refused to turn and look at the television vans as she hurried to the door.

An SUV was coming through the parking lot, as well.

It was cool inside the market, and someone was adjusting the piped-in music. Lisa got a cart and passed Joseph Martinelli building a display of boxed macaroni dinners. "Morning," the store employee said.

"Morning."

Lisa decided to stock up on nonperishables so she wouldn't have to come back for a while. She filled her cart quickly and headed for the checkout, where she glanced with trepidation toward the magazine racks. None of them sported her picture, of course, but she sympathized with Kirstie Alley, who'd been photographed at her least flattering moments. She pushed her cart on past.

The two women checkers spotted her and one said something to the other. Lisa had seen both of them in here for years and neither had ever voiced more than the total of her purchase.

Today, however, the woman checking her out said, "Beautiful morning, isn't it?"

Lisa nodded.

"Did you find everything you needed? This is the best buy this week. I got some of these nectarines the other day and my son loved them."

"They do look good." Lisa dug in her wallet for her debit card.

When she glanced up, a tall, dark-haired man was making a purchase in the other lane. She'd recognize Riley Douglas anywhere, even without his sport jacket. Buying his own groceries? How unlikely was that?

He accepted a plastic bag from the checker and turned to leave, then noticed her.

The woman was bagging Lisa's groceries.

"Well, hi," he said easily. "You're out early."

"Had to get my worms."

He gave her a blank look.

"Never mind. What brings you into town?"

He raised his bag, which clearly held only one small item. "Allergies are kicking up. Had to pick up something."

And he didn't have a prescription for that? Or a personal assistant to run his errands? He looked fine to her. No watering, itchy eyes or runny nose that she detected.

"Uh-huh. Well, I hope it does the trick."

"Carryout on five, please," the checker called.

"I'll get this," Riley said and took charge of the cart. Lisa glanced from the woman to Riley's back and followed him and her groceries out the door.

"You realize you're on *Candid Camera*," she said as they crossed the parking lot.

He glanced toward the media vehicles. "Not so candid. Is it like this everywhere you go?"

"Pretty much. They'll probably go in and interview the checker now, and tonight's news will feature my supper menu."

"Yeah, how was the pizza last night?"

She blinked. "You read that this morning?"

With a grin, he nodded.

They had reached Lisa's Blazer, and she used the key to unlock the back door. It opened with a squeak of metal, and a few flakes of rust fell to the pavement.

"I got rear-ended once," she said. "This door's never been the same." She'd used the insurance money to pay her vet bill instead of having the dent pounded out, but she didn't feel the need to share that detail.

Riley set her bags in the back, glancing at the items on top. "What kind of wine goes with rawhide strips?"

"Those aren't my dinner."

"No kidding." He finished loading her groceries and pushed the cart into a return area. "Have you been to the mine yet?"

She shook her head. Oddly enough, she wasn't even sure where the Queen of Hearts was located.

"Want to take a ride out there and have a look at your property?"

Couldn't hurt, could it? She'd been curious but too self-conscious of the stares. She gestured with her thumb to indicate their observers. "They'll follow, you know."

Riley didn't look toward the media vans. "We could lose them."

"How?"

He appeared to be thinking for a moment. "Drive out to my place. They'll follow. We'll leave your vehicle parked and take another one."

"But they'll see us leave."

"Trust me. I'll figure it out."

She shrugged. "Okay. I have to get my groceries home, then take care of a few pets. It might take me a couple hours."

He reached into his pocket and took out a tiny phone, which he flipped open. "What's your cell phone number?"

"Don't have one."

He closed the phone. "Do you have a piece of paper?"

She rummaged through her purse and found a receipt and a pen.

He jotted something down and handed both back. "That's mine. Call me when you're leaving."

She put the pen and note in her purse and got into her car.

An hour and a half later, none of the dogs questioned had answered when asked if they were having any allergy symptoms.

She stopped by the McGills' to feed their cats and change litter boxes. She asked Sassy and Callie about allergies, as well, but after being rudely ignored, she returned home, freshened up and made an attempt to tame her hair.

If she changed clothes, Riley would think she was

trying to impress him or that she cared what he thought. She wasn't and she didn't, so she wore what she had on.

Lisa called Bernadine to make sure she wasn't making a tactical error. "I'm going to see the mine site with Riley Douglas. Do you think there's a problem with that?"

"Sounds innocent enough. Unless he tries to get you to sign something. Or tries to get you naked."

Warmth infused Lisa's cheeks even though she was alone. "I wouldn't sign anything. And he's not going to try to…do the other thing you said. What made you think that?"

"You're a rich woman now. Some men find that very attractive, if you know what I mean."

"I do know and I'll be wary."

"If I was you, I'd be expecting men to fall all over me."

"Thanks for the warning, but it's not like I don't suspect ulterior motives. Let's see, last ten years, no men seeking me out. Now, today, suddenly man pays attention. I can figure it out."

"Okay. Good."

Her next call was to Riley to let him know she was leaving her house.

Lisa would rather have believed Riley was just a nice guy offering to help, but their history made her assume otherwise. She drove to the Lazy D, followed by the news vans. They parked out on the road when she pulled into his drive.

Riley led her out the back door, where his assistant, Marge, waited in the driver's seat of a Lexus. "Get down in the front," he told her, and she ducked down on the passenger side while he got into the rear and did the same.

Feeling as if she'd been zapped into an old *Dukes of Hazzard* rerun, she prayed Marge wouldn't be driving through fields or jumping any waterways. "Where are we going?"

"I'm taking you to the garage at the big house," Marge replied. "I come and go from this place all day long, so no one will think anything of it."

A few minutes of blissfully sedate driving later, they pulled into a darkened building, and an automatic door lowered.

"Thanks, Marge," Riley told the woman.

She smiled and handed Lisa a straw hat. "Anytime."

Riley led Lisa to a red sports car, held the door for her and, after pressing a garage-door opener, guided the car out into the daylight. "Put that hat on."

"If we're avoiding the newspeople, I shouldn't need it." She tossed the hat on the backseat.

No cars followed as Riley took a back road. "This way is longer, but we'll avoid the cameras."

"Works for me."

She couldn't help noticing the shape of his long fingers on the gearshift or the way his jeans stretched taut over his thighs as he drove. He was as appealing as he'd been in high school, sexier even, and the fact wasn't lost on her. That *naked* word that Bernadine had used still disturbed her, especially when she thought it in his presence.

Riley knew a back route that brought them out farther north on Thunder Canyon Road. He headed south.

"One of the first things on my agenda was to have a chain-link fence built around the entire area, including the sinkhole and the mine entrance, to protect all the land where the mine sits."

"Think it's necessary?"

"Would you lock up a million dollars or leave it out?"

"Good point."

He took an unmarked road. Four times, brown-uniformed men stationed along the way stopped the car, and each time Riley showed his identification. It wasn't long before they reached the entrance to the mine.

Two more uniformed men walked out of a canopy-style tent and approached the car. Lisa was surprised to see them carrying pistols in shoulder holsters. Their belts held walkie-talkies and nightsticks. "Looks like they're ready for an invasion."

Riley walked around to open her door, but she'd already stepped out.

"Mr. Douglas," one of the uniformed men greeted him. "I didn't recognize the car."

"We're incognito."

The guard looked Lisa over then, and recognition dawned. "Gotcha."

"Miss Martin's come to look over her property."

"It's been quiet all week," the man told them.

"That's what we like to hear."

The entrance to the mine had obviously once been completely closed up, but boards had been removed and replaced with steel beams to take the load from aging timbers.

"Is it safe?" she asked.

"Up front, it is. It's only been shored up for six hundred feet so far. We won't go farther than that."

He entered a trailer situated nearby and returned with two yellow hard hats with lights affixed and carried a high-powered flashlight. He handed Lisa one of the hats, which she placed on her head, then he led the way into the mine.

The beams from their hats bounced off the walls, creating bouncing shadows as they entered and looked around. The interior was larger and cooler than she'd expected, and lights had been strung from posts. It was obvious that a lot of work had already been done to add support and safety features. As the tunnel led them increasingly deeper and lower, their steps echoed eerily in the stillness. Lisa imagined the primitive conditions that had once existed and pictured the original owner, whoever he'd been, carving out these walls.

They walked as far as the improvements extended, and Lisa stared into the yawning darkness beyond. Nothing glittered or gleamed or screamed *gold* to her, and the musty-earth smell was stronger. Growing up, she'd read too many Nancy Drew novels to feel comfortable in the bowels of a mine. "So, somewhere in there is a lot of gold, eh?"

Her voice carried through the darkness in a ghostly echo. It took all her courage not to move closer to Riley.

"That's right," he replied, speaking softly. The low timber of his voice sent a shiver up her spine. "A vein was discovered when a rescue worker was found with the nugget after Erik Stevenson fell into the mine a few months ago. Our experts' analysis showed the vein stretches back at least another three hundred feet beyond what's been exposed and branches considerably downward."

"And this mine was thought to be played out?"

"Apparently. And forgotten over the years."

"I wonder how my great-great-grandmother came to own it."

"Apparently her father, Bart, was the second owner. He may have purchased it or won it in a card game. No way to know for sure. Upon his death, she inherited it."

"Wasn't there a story about Lily losing the mine to your ancestor?"

"One story says she owed money to Amos Douglas and he took the land as payment."

"And the other?"

"The other says he foreclosed on her property and took it."

"Aren't there records?"

"That was over a hundred years ago. People didn't exactly have to keep information for income taxes."

"So how did the fact that I owned the deed come to light?"

"Emily Stanton and Brad Vaughn did all the digging on that. Apparently, as one of their last efforts, they had a talk with Tildy Matheson."

Lisa knew who the old woman was.

"Her grandmother was good friends with Amos's wife, Catherine. Tildy offered to show them papers and pictures that had been in her attic, and among her grandmother's things was the deed to the mine—signed back over to Lily Divine Harding."

Lisa glanced up at Riley. It was difficult to see his expression with the light on his hat glaring into the darkness. "And that's a legal document?"

"More legal than anything we Douglases can come up with."

She'd displaced him from ownership of a gold mine. "And how do you feel about that?"

He seemed surprised at her question and didn't immediately form a reply.

"Sorry. Dumb question."

"No. I just didn't want to sound insincere when I answered."

She noticed he didn't say he didn't want to *be* insincere, just that he didn't want to *sound* that way.

"Let's head back," he said and directed the flashlight beam back the way they'd come. He moved around her, brushing her shoulder with his chest. The heat from his body was a pleasant surprise in the cool interior of the mine. "I tried every way I knew to prove ownership to the land. I couldn't do it. You're the owner. Those are the facts."

And on the surface he'd been helpful and informative rather than resentful. The darkness at her back made her uncomfortable, and she didn't let him get too far ahead of her. "What's in this for you?"

He glanced at her, and she had to squint against the beam of light. He reached up and switched it off, then did the same to hers. "I've offered to manage your business. You're coming into a lot of money. If I work for you, I'll make money, too. Plain and simple."

Sounded too plain and simple. Maybe Bernadine was right.

Lisa blinked as they reached the mouth of the mine and the bright sunlight. While Riley returned their hats to the trailer, she found her sunglasses in her purse and slipped them on.

Riley drove her back to his place, where she thanked him, then headed home in her Blazer. There was more that she needed to know. She knew very little about her ancestor. Legend had it that Lily had run a bordello in Thunder Canyon, and apparently the museum held historical artifacts from that time. In all these years Lisa had never visited. She'd never wanted anyone to see her there.

There was one less news vehicle across from her house when she reached it, and she took that as a good sign that things were settling down.

That night the clips of her at the Super Saver Mart were brief, and the anchorwoman moved right along to a story about a grant for the library and a literacy program.

Lisa peered out her front window as her pork chop cooked on her indoor ceramic grill. She was boring, anyone could see that. Eventually they had to lose interest and move on. She wasn't going to suddenly do something exciting.

She had more meetings scheduled the next day, and Bernadine would be picking her up. Maybe afterward she could slip away unnoticed to go to the museum.

That evening she planned her escape and packed a canvas tote bag with a change of clothing and a scarf.

The following afternoon Lisa wished Bernadine goodbye and slipped into the restroom of the courthouse, where they'd been filing papers. She changed clothes, tied the scarf around her hair bandanna-style and put on her sunglasses like a spy in a James Bond movie.

She exited the building through a back door and walked several blocks to the museum, which used to be an old schoolhouse. The building was centered on an acre of land that had once been the school yard. Lisa glanced in both directions, but no one had followed her.

She entered the reception area.

A woman greeted her. "Do you have a membership?"

"No."

"Admission is six dollars."

Lisa paid the amount and accepted a brochure.

"As you enter, the room to your left holds displays of mining equipment and information about the history of Thunder Canyon and local industry. There's a Native American display and a pioneer-life section.

"As you see, in the center area are groupings of furniture arranged to look as they may have at one time."

Lisa glanced at the roped-off sections, her gaze wandering toward what she really wanted to locate.

"The room to the right holds personal items used by our town founders and the more infamous inhabitants of Thunder Canyon. Enjoy your visit. If I can be of any assistance, just ask. Please sign the guest book and visit our gift shop before you leave. All proceeds go to the historical society to support the museum."

"I will, thanks." Lisa wanted to head directly for the room on the right, but instead she nonchalantly moseyed among the pieces of furniture, entered the large room on the left and studied the displays.

The picks and scales and claim deeds were of timely interest since she'd just seen the inside of her first mine. Black-and-white photographs, enlarged and displayed on foam board, brought the miners to life with real faces. Someone, once upon a long-ago time—probably her ancestor, Bart Divine—had toiled in the depths of the Queen of Hearts with sweat and hope and then had apparently given up. She was curious about those times and increasingly curious about Lily.

The museum lady was nowhere to be seen and no other visitors were in the building when Lisa peeked across the center room. She made her way past settings of chairs and sideboards and a cast-iron stove holding a kettle to enter the opposite room.

A quick survey showed her the window she'd come to see, and she hurried closer. A mannequin dressed in a dance-hall costume stood to one side in the exhibit. The red satin dress was trimmed with black lace and had been scandalously revealing for its time. Long ropes of pearls hung around the mannequin's bare neck, and a black ostrich feather had been affixed to the dark wig.

Lisa drew her gaze to the objects displayed in the case and their descriptions: a tortoiseshell hair comb studded with rhinestones, several perfume bottles, a fan edged with Chantilly lace and trimmed with black purling braid and a fancy pair of black silk garters, each with a gilt buckle and a rosette of satin taffeta ribbon.

Her attention was drawn to a pair of photographs. One was of the inside of the infamous Shady Lady saloon. A bartender in a white shirt with black armbands stood behind the polished mahogany bar. On the wall behind the bar were rows of liquor bottles and glasses, and center stage was a painting.

The caption under the photo claimed that the portrait

was of none other than Lily Divine herself. The likeness was too small for Lisa to make out any features, but the most obvious thing to note was that the woman who had posed for the portrait was bare except for something sheer draped across her hip and hiding only minimal secrets.

Lisa read that the painting was property of the Hitching Post and still hung over the bar. She'd heard talk of the portrait before, of course. In high school, coarse comments had been made, along with inquiries as to whether she was as stacked as Lily Divine, but she'd been too embarrassed to go see for herself.

The last photograph was a picture of her great-great-grandmother. Dark-haired and fair of features, she stood on the white-painted stairs of a house, dressed in a very average-looking skirt and a blouse with a high lace collar. She shaded her eyes with one hand and wore a gentle smile.

Her expression struck Lisa as one of a woman sure of herself. Confident. Poised. A woman who knew her place in her world.

Somehow those qualities had been lost in the gene pool, she thought. Lisa stared at the picture for a long time. In all these years she'd never come here because she'd been embarrassed. Ashamed of Lily Divine's reputation and legacy. Her aunt and grandmother had rarely spoken of the woman, and when they had it had been in lowered tones of disapproval.

Lisa tried to make sense of Lily being friends with Amos Douglas's wife. If Lily had run a house of ill repute and Amos Douglas had been an upstanding forefather, how had the two women been acquainted?

There was more here than she was able to see on the surface. A big piece of the puzzle was missing, and something drove her to discover what that was. Maybe her own visit to Tildy Matheson was in order.

Chapter Four

"Riley, I didn't know you were coming by again today." Caleb Douglas spotted his son at the computer in the adjoining office. They had remodeled this downtown building where all the business for the ski-resort project was handled, but Riley worked from his home office most of the time.

"I needed to crunch a few numbers."

Ground-breaking for Thunder Canyon Resort had been set back by the gold-fever commotion and subsequent land disputes but was back on schedule.

The older man entered the room and closed the door behind him. Riley's mother had obviously chosen the shirt and tie Caleb wore, which coordinated with his tailor-made western-cut sport jacket. Caleb stepped in front of Riley's desk. "How are things going with the Martin girl?"

"She's about to hire me."

"You're going to have to push this a little faster. One more 9/11 scare will send gold sky-high. We need to be in place when that happens."

"It's coming together."

"The mining is moving forward. There's gonna be gold coming out of that hole by the ton."

"I said I'm working on it."

Caleb held up both hands. "Okay. It had better be good." He started to walk away, then stopped as if he'd had a thought.

"I'm meeting Justin for lunch. Care to join us?"

Justin Caldwell was the brother Riley hadn't known about until a month ago. Justin, however, had learned about Caleb two years previously and had schemed against the Douglases to get control of the ski resort through the investors. His scheme had worked, too. The manipulation and resulting takeover had nearly broken Caleb. But in the end Justin had experienced a change of heart and given control of the project back to Caleb. Now the two of them seemed to be downright bonding.

Riley grabbed a pen and jotted down a few numbers. "I have other plans."

"Well, that's a shame. I'd like to get my two boys together for a change."

"Yeah, that would be real nice."

"Riley, he married our girl, Katie. You're going to have to accept him."

Riley's parents had taken in Katie Fenton when she'd

been fourteen and her mother had died. Katie's mother and Adele had been college friends. Katie was the daughter Caleb never had, his darling. Riley had been in college at the time, but he'd grown to love her, too. More often than not, however—even though he was the only offspring from his parents' union—he felt like the outsider in the family.

"Your mother's talking about a get-together soon," Caleb said. "A family thing. Bring someone."

Riley watched his father leave the room. Finding out about Justin had been a shock. His father'd had an affair when Riley had been just a baby. Justin had been the result of that, and Riley and his mother were still coming to terms with the betrayal.

Adele was a strong, proud woman, and her position in the community stiffened her backbone when it came to handling tough conditions. Riley, too, was loyal to family and the Douglas name. He and Justin had formed a tentative relationship, but Riley still had issues.

Not liking it didn't change the situation. He'd worked hard for his position in the Douglas Corporation and he wasn't going to let any of that go to waste. His plan was already in motion.

Lisa found Matilda Matheson in the Thunder Canyon phone directory and called her to set up a visit. The woman had been warm and friendly on the phone and sounded eager to meet her.

The following morning after her a.m. dogs were walked and fed, Lisa drove to the library, changed her clothing in the restroom and left by the rear door, wearing the only pair of trousers she owned and a hooded sweatshirt. These devious evasion tactics were getting old fast.

Her destination was a fair distance, but she was used to walking and no one spotted her. The house she sought was a two-story blue-and-white Victorian in excellent condition. Roses climbed trellises on either side of the porch and a calico cat napped on the padded porch swing.

Tildy was a kindly old woman with a toothy smile and soft-looking gray hair. She welcomed Lisa into her parlor and offered her a seat on the floral-cushioned sofa. Crocheted antimacassars were pinned to the arms and backs of the pieces of furniture.

"I'm tickled pink to meet you, dear. I've got tea ready. It won't be a moment."

Lisa glanced around, noting vintage furnishings and lamps similar in age and condition to those in her home.

Tildy came back with tea and sugar cookies. The china was delicate rose-patterned chintz with worn gold trim.

"I'm ever so pleased to meet Lily Divine's great-great-granddaughter," she said, clasping her hands together at her breast. "But I'm curious to know what brings you here."

"I understand your grandmother was a friend of Catherine Douglas's."

"Oh, yes, dear. The two were confidantes."

"Emily Stanton shared some of the story with me. The part about how she and Brad came to discover the deed to the mine."

"That was a surprise to all of us. I'm delighted for

you, dear. Those Douglases don't need any more money and they certainly don't deserve the mine."

"Why's that?"

"Well, the way my grandmother told the story, Amos Douglas was a mean old coot, who beat Catherine on more than one occasion. Lily was always the one who took her in and nursed her to health."

Lisa tried to picture a woman in a red saloon dress sitting at Catherine Douglas's bedside but couldn't make the scene gel.

"It wasn't unusual for her to take in women who needed a safe place."

"And a brothel was a safe place?" Lisa asked with serious doubt.

Tildy waved away that idea with a frown. "My grandmother said the Shady Lady was a dance hall, not a house of ill repute. Still, as a saloon it was not a place where respectable women of that day would have worked."

"But all the stories and the Heritage Day celebrations portray Lily as a prostitute."

"Makes for a far more colorful legend and a more interesting historical character that way, don't you think?"

Lisa recalled the face of the woman in the old photograph at the museum and the ordinary high-necked blouse and skirt she'd been wearing. She could picture that woman taking in an abused wife. "How can I know the truth from fiction?"

"I don't know, dear. You're welcome to go through Catherine's things. Emily and Brad left the trunk in my extra bedroom. It was in my attic for years before they brought it down here."

"Thank you, Miss Matheson. I'd like that."

Tildy sat in a rocker before a lace-curtained window in the quaintly decorated bedroom while Lisa looked through the contents of the enormous trunk. The fabric of the old dresses was so fragile, she feared tearing it, so she moved it aside carefully. She found a tarnished silver hand mirror, a parasol and a faded green silk purse.

"I intend to donate these things to the historical society, but somehow I just don't get around to calling them," Tildy told her. "My grandmother inherited all of Catherine's belongings, and I've had them since I was a young girl." Her hand went to a brooch she wore on her flowered dress. "I've worn the pieces of jewelry all my life."

"I'm the same way with my grandmother's things," Lisa told her. "I've kept most everything."

"The trunk and its contents are in my will," the old woman told her. "The foundation will get them when I'm gone."

Lisa didn't know how to respond, so she smiled and nodded. Catherine had kept several journals, and she read the first few entries in one.

"You may borrow those if you like. I'm sure there's mention of Lily."

Lisa ran her hand across the aged and cracked leather cover of the book she held. "I'll be very careful with them."

"I know you will, dear." Tildy wrapped the journals in tissue paper and placed them in a small bag for Lisa to carry.

After another cup of tea and more of the best cookies she'd ever eaten, Lisa thanked Tildy and left her house. On the walk back to the library she experienced a wash of anger that those stories of Lily's supposed profession had been propagated over the years. Because of another woman's hypothetical lack of moral character, Lisa had been looked down on her whole life—when all along that could have been one big lie!

If there was a way to absolve Lily's name, she was going to try to find it.

The back door of the library was locked when she arrived, so she had to walk around front to get to her Blazer. Only one news van remained, and the driver appeared to be napping. Lisa started the engine and drove away without a tail.

She felt blissfully unencumbered when she stopped and took care of her afternoon pets, then drove home.

She let herself in and the dogs licked her senseless, then danced around yipping until she put leashes on them and took them out for a walk. The driver of a news van spotted her on her return and drove slowly alongside. "I'm reporting you to the police," she called. "I have a restraining order!"

The van dropped back and she hurried on to the house.

That evening she curled up on the sofa with one of the journals and read it from the beginning. It had been written during an early time in Catherine's life, and there was no mention of Lily. The second book, however, mentioned Lily a few times, referring to her home as a refuge. The dates of the entries were sporadic, and Lisa had the impression that Catherine had left out much of the true happenings of her life.

Emily had given Lisa her phone number, and Lisa

called it now, only to get a recording. Emily and Brad had done extensive research in looking for the mine owner, and perhaps she had discovered more than Lisa had thought to ask about.

She left a message, then tried to distract herself by baking brownies. Her grandmother's recipes were some of her dearest treasures, and these brownies especially reminded her of the warmth and comfort she'd received in this home during her formative years. Lisa poured herself a glass of milk and ate the brownies warm.

Emily might not return her call for hours or perhaps not even until the next day. She dusted the china hutch and sideboard in the dining room, admiring the dishes and thinking how similar her grandmother's things were to Tildy's. She still missed her grandmother, even though she'd been gone several years. Having her things was a comfort, just as the house was her link to family. Maybe part of the reason she was so curious about Lily was because she craved a family connection.

Later, as she was washing up the baking dishes, the phone rang.

"Hi, Lisa, it's Emily. I got your message."

"Thanks for calling. I have a couple of questions and I thought you could help me find answers."

"If I can, sure."

"I went to see Tildy today."

"She's a sweetheart, isn't she?"

"And the cookies are to die for."

Emily chuckled.

"She doesn't believe Lily Divine ran a whorehouse. Her grandmother told her differently."

"I got that impression, too. Of course, there's no official documentation to prove it one way or the other."

Lisa propped the phone under her chin and dried a spatula. "I guess prostitutes didn't exactly apply for a license to practice, did they?"

"It was a lucrative business back then. The saloons supported the city. In fact, the law often accepted payment to simply look aside."

Lisa thought about that. "And the lawmen probably frequented the places."

"Likely. It was a western mining town. Saloon owners got rich off the miners."

"Did you learn anything else about Lily?"

"Brad and I searched all the papers in the archives in the town-hall basement."

"That must have been fun."

"Actually it wasn't so bad. Lily's name came up a lot in later years, when she was Lily Harding. She was married to the town sheriff."

That news surprised Lisa. She leaned back against the counter. "I thought that was probably another tall tale."

"No. She was married to Nathaniel Harding, who by many accounts brought law and order to Thunder Canyon. Lily herself was a voice ahead of her time, speaking out for women's rights and later in their quest for the vote."

"You found articles in the *Nugget* that told about that?"

"We did."

"I think I'm going to go look through them myself."

"That's a good idea. We weren't really searching for

Lily's history, so there may have been information we overlooked."

"Thanks, Emily."

"Anytime. How are things going?"

"What? You don't know? I thought my menu and routine were public knowledge."

Emily laughed. I know about the pizza, but I was actually wondering about *you*. Are you handling all this?"

"It's pretty awful. I can't go anywhere without cameras following. I'm my own reality show and I'm boring. I did make some awesome brownies tonight."

"They'll find something else to interest them soon and you'll be old news."

"Not soon enough for me. Thanks again."

"Oh," Emily added, "one more thing I just thought of."

"What's that?"

"There's an elderly woman who lives out on the western edge of town, past Elk. Almost to the Douglas property."

"Emelda Ross," Lisa said. "She reads to the children at the library."

"That's her," Emily said. "You've met her?"

"Used to go to story time when I was a kid. My mother took me."

"Well, anyway, she has stories about the early days of Thunder Canyon that just don't quit. She was quite entertaining when I spoke with her. She might know more about Lily."

"Maybe I'll go see her. Thanks." Lisa hung up and glanced at the clock. It was too late to go visiting, but she would make a trip out to the Ross house soon.

* * *

They'd caught on. The next morning Lisa opened the back door at the library, and farther down the alley two reporters who'd been leaning against the fenders of their vehicles grabbed cameras and aimed the lenses at her.

"Come on, people! There has to be something going on *somewhere* that's more interesting than this." She went back inside and stood in the hall a moment.

She changed plans and walked out the front door and down Main. She didn't turn to look behind her, but she knew the vans were back there. All the buildings along Main Street sat side by side with covered boardwalks. When she reached Town Hall, the receptionist, a woman with black hair and a white streak over one temple, recognized her and accompanied her to the records in the basement. She showed her the basic layout and how to get started finding newspaper articles.

For a couple of hours Lisa scanned microfiche of the *Thunder Canyon Nugget.* More than once Lily had spent the night in jail for refusing to turn a woman over to her husband or father. Most of those incidents had been before Nathaniel Harding became sheriff, Lisa noted. There was only one account of the sheriff actually locking up the woman he would marry. One story told of a fire that had ravaged a property Lily owned, and there was mention of an auction Lily held to raise money for a fatherless family.

Again Lisa thought of the woman she'd seen in the black-and-white photograph. *Confident* had been her overall impression of Lily. Assured of her purpose.

Comfortable with her life choices. There was no doubt she'd owned and run a saloon. In fact, according to announcements in the *Nugget,* numerous town meetings had been held in her establishment.

Lily'd held her own in a time when women were considered inferior. Nothing inferior about Lily Divine. She'd raised her head high and marched to her own tune.

Lisa marched to her own tune, as well, but it was a quiet melody, written to blend into the surrounding sounds. She'd spent her whole life trying to be invisible.

She hated attention, and why was that? Was she inferior to others in some respect? Looks? Money? Yes. Yes.

Well, she had money now. Or at least she would have. Bernadine was rushing the paperwork. The Douglases had established an account to hold future profits from sales of ore from the Queen of Hearts, and the names were already being changed on that account. The thought of being responsible for a prospective million dollars or more plus employees and all that this inheritance entailed made her feel ill. She definitely needed all the help she could get.

Lisa walked out the front door of Town Hall and spotted the news vans. She was disgusted with herself for hiding because she felt inferior. She could hide because she didn't want the publicity, but feeling inferior was wrong.

Instead of heading back for her Blazer, she headed west on Main until she came to the Hitching Post. Old Town had been restored and reconstructed to look like the 1800s town it had once been, and true to the bar and restaurant's name, split-rail hitching posts lined the boardwalk.

Two cars were parked in front, and she glanced at her watch, noting it wasn't yet the lunch hour. The place was popular and would probably fill up with locals soon.

Her stomach fluttered as she opened the door and entered the building with unexpected awe. The Hitching Post had been here for forty years in its current form and sixty-plus years before the remodeling. Her great-great-grandmother had stood on these very floors and walked the same rooms and lived and slept in the attached house next door.

The floors were scarred wood, the varnished pine walls darkened over the years. Lanterns, tin signs, spurs and all number of western memorabilia hung from nails and dangled in the doorways. How many of these walls and items had Lily touched?

No one stood near the counter at the front, and Lisa could see the bar from the entrance. The sound of a slow ballad droned from a jukebox in the corner. Two silver-haired men played checkers at a table and a stocky, middle-aged man in a white shirt stacked glasses behind the bar.

Lisa recognized the enormous polished cherrywood bar from the photograph and approached. The piece was hopelessly scarred and several grooves had been worn deep in the wood, but it was still impressive. Behind the bar, in a place of prominence between mirrors and shelves of glasses and rows of liquor bottles, was the painting she'd come to see.

The place didn't get a whole lot of sunlight, which had

probably aided in preserving the portrait. It was bigger than she'd anticipated, but every bit as…provocative.

Clearly the same Lily Divine that she'd seen in the photograph was depicted in the artist's rendition. Reclining on her side, the woman faced the artist. If Lisa wasn't mistaken, Lily's curly dark hair had the same auburn highlights as her own, and similar ringlets framed her face. The similarity was as surprising as it was exciting. What other characteristics did they share?

This Lily had probably been in her twenties and was depicted adorned with…pearls. Period. Lisa definitely wore more clothing.

The woman wasn't the well-rounded type Lisa'd seen in nude paintings in art-history books, although she obviously had what it took in all the right places. No wonder Lisa'd been asked how she compared to Lily Divine. The chick *was* stacked.

Her breasts were clearly visible through a gauzy black veil that draped over one shoulder, and Victoria's Secret would have signed this woman in a heartbeat. The material gathered over her hip and discreetly shaded her pubic area.

Lily's legs were long and shapely, and strands of pearls circled each ankle. Lily Divine was a hottie.

"This your first look at the Shady Lady?"

"What?" Lisa glanced at the bartender who'd approached. "Oh, yes."

"We got postcards we sell to the tourists if you wanna buy one." He pointed to a rack on the counter by an ice machine. "A dollar. Want one?"

"Sure, thanks." She opened her purse.

He placed a postcard on the bar. "What'll you have to drink?"

"Um." She glanced at the card and then around the interior of the room, orienting herself. "Do you have root beer?"

He shook his head. "Cola."

"Diet?"

"Sure thing." He prepared her a glass of soda and set it on a cocktail napkin. "Two fifty with the postcard."

She paid him, and he gave her another look, recognition dawning. "Say, aren't you…?"

Lisa's cheeks warmed and she busied herself placing the picture in her purse.

The man snapped his fingers. "You're the heiress." His eyebrows shot up. "The gal who inherited the gold mine!"

She acknowledged his observation with a nod and the bravest smile she could come up with. "That's me."

"Then you're—" He stopped and pointed up at the painting. "You're the Shady Lady's kin."

She looked back up at the portrait. It had hung there for generations. No sense getting embarrassed about it now. She was after all linked through history to this establishment. "That's right."

"Well…congratulations."

She nodded her thanks and he moved away. Lisa sipped her soft drink while she studied the portrait. What a fascinating woman Lily had been. She'd been known down through the years as the Shady Lady, though there wasn't much proof that she'd been a prostitute. Actually this painting seemed to be the only tie to her not-so-proper past.

What exactly had the woman had to be ashamed of?

Not that body, that was for sure. Though the painting must have been scandalous in its day, one could see nearly as much flesh today watching a Super Bowl halftime.

The artist had captured Lily's expression so vividly that this was without a doubt the same confident woman as the one in the photograph at the museum. Her dauntless smile revealed her pleasure with life. Perhaps pleasure with herself or her accomplishments.

Lisa wanted the same confidence Lily had possessed. Why hadn't she inherited that? She wondered then about Lily's children and what had transpired down through the generations to make Lisa and her great-great-grandmother so different.

"Want something else?" the bartender asked, snagging her attention.

She'd finished her soft drink. "No, thanks. I'll be moving along."

She picked up her purse and left the Hitching Post. A couple of her paparazzi were out of their vehicles, chatting in the shade of a maple tree. They saw her and jumped to their positions to follow. She observed them for a moment and wondered what Lily would have done if she'd been in this same predicament.

It was several blocks back to the library where she'd parked, but instead of hurrying, she took her time. Along the way she passed the Clip 'N' Curl salon. She'd always thought it sounded like a place where you'd take your poodle, but it was the only hair salon in town. Judy Johnson usually cut Lisa's hair.

Lisa had gone to school with Judy's daughter, Jennifer, so she always got an update on Jennifer's charmed and perfect life with her charmed and perfect teacher husband and her charmed and perfect children—one girl and one boy, of course.

Lisa pushed open the door and the overhead bell rang. The smell of perming solution immediately burned her nostrils. One customer in rods was being neutralized and two others sat under dryers. A fourth was having her silver-blue hair styled into waves.

"Hello, Lisa," Judy called. "I'm doing a perm and a color, so it'll be another hour."

"That's okay. I'll come back."

She stood on the boardwalk and glanced up and down the street before continuing on to her vehicle.

As she drove home, she changed her mind about going back to the Clip 'N' Curl. She'd try something different for a change. If she thought her Blazer would make it, she'd drive to Billings and visit a salon. Or a day spa.

Some millionaire she was. She didn't even have a decent car.

Joey and Piper wagged their tails excitedly when she arrived, and she knelt to give them both attention before letting them out into the backyard.

The light on the answering machine was blinking, and the contraption actually cooperated, so she played her messages. One was from Bernadine saying she needed a few signatures. Another was from someone named Dave who claimed they'd gone to school together and was wondering if she'd like to hook up. She remembered him as the receiver on the football team. He'd sat beside her in Language Arts and had never so much as spoken to her.

The last recording made her heartbeat stutter when she heard the deep male voice. *The quarterback.*

"Lisa, this is Riley. Give me a call when you get in. I want to ask you something. Later."

She used great discipline in phoning Bernadine first and arranged for a quick meeting. Then she took the slip of paper on which Riley'd written his cell phone number and dialed.

"Hey, you called me back."

"Yes. You wanted to ask me something?"

"I did. Will you have dinner with me Friday evening? We can drive into Billings. I'll make reservations somewhere nice."

Was this a business dinner? Or…personal? Her stomach dipped. She wasn't into the whole dating scene, and if he was expecting her to be cute or coy, it wasn't going to happen.

"Is this…business?"

"Do you want it to be?"

"I just don't want to mess up our relationship as client and agent."

"You haven't hired me yet."

"Right. Well, you're hired." She paused a moment. "Now we have a working relationship."

"Good. So I'll pick you up Friday?"

She still didn't know his intent, but she surprised herself and said okay anyway. She hung up the phone and second-guessed herself while she looked for something to eat for lunch. Dinner at someplace nice. Just thinking about it almost made her lose her appetite. What would she wear?

Maybe she would go to Billings and do a little shopping. She had credit cards. She could even rent a decent car to get there. She was a millionaire, after all. Excited about the idea, she slapped together a peanut-butter sandwich.

Chapter Five

Lisa glanced around the inside of the New Beginnings Day Spa searching for someone who looked like exactly the person she wanted cutting her hair. She spotted her giving a man in his twenties a cut. "Her."

"That's Miranda. Five minutes, hon."

Miranda had short hair, dark at the roots and a combination of blonde and red on the bleached ends. She wore black high-heeled boots and dangling rhinestone earrings.

"I don't want to look like the old me," Lisa told her ten minutes later. "I need a whole new look."

"What are you going for? Color? Surprise?"

"Anything will be a surprise. I just want to feel good. I want to be…confident."

Miranda washed and conditioned her hair, combed

it back from her face and studied her. "Can I do your eyebrows?"

"Sure."

"You have a great face. I want to give you a look you can learn to do yourself. I can give you a good cut, just above your shoulders and sort of fringy around your face. We'll do some highlights to add depth. And I can teach you to straighten it yourself. Wait till you see the results."

Miranda went to work. She was serious about her job and about the look she wanted Lisa to achieve. She snipped and cut and colored, and Lisa began to have a few qualms about what she'd gotten herself into. She didn't want to look foolish when all was done.

Her fears were soon put to rest when the hairdresser spun her around in the chair to face the mirror. The pretty young woman she stared at didn't look anything like the frumpy old Lisa. No frizz, just shine and soft curl that flattered the shape of her face.

Lisa had picked a miracle worker. The result was amazing.

Lisa studied her reflection and couldn't believe the difference. "I love it."

But they weren't done. Miranda worked with her until she could use the products and the iron and get her hair straight and styled on her own.

"Now," Miranda said. "Makeup."

"I do okay."

"No argument. You said you don't want to look like the old you. You need a face for the new you."

"You're right."

"I'll go get the cosmetologist."

Makeup was one thing. Waxing was entirely another. But Lisa'd come for the day and the works and she was going to stay for the whole ride. Legs waxed, a manicure, pedicure and a signature on a credit-card slip later and she was headed for a shop several blocks away where the stylist had recommended she go.

Lisa entered the store, which had two levels and a main sitting area with a cappuccino machine. A slim young woman in a fashionable blouse and skirt greeted her.

"I'm Gwen. Miranda told me you were coming. You look fabulous. I have a few things I'd like you to try on. Did you have anything specific in mind?"

"Actually I did. I think I'd like something in red."

Bernadine nearly fell out of her office chair the next day when Lisa walked in after the secretary's announcement over the intercom. "Lisa? Oh, my gosh! You look *fabulous!* It is you, isn't it?"

"It's me." She did a little whirl before the woman's desk, showing off her trim two-piece suit and sexy backless heels. It was a completely new experience to feel attractive, and she was enjoying the feeling.

Bernadine got up to come around and stare, hands on her cheeks.

"Big change, huh?"

"Change? My word, more like a total metamorphosis! You're like one of those extreme makeovers." She reached up to touch a wisp of Lisa's hair. "This color is incredible."

"I was pretty bad, wasn't I?"

The woman looked embarrassed. "No, well, not ugly or anything, just…well, okay, not a very fashionable dresser and, um…. Not bad, though."

"It's okay. I know."

Bernadine inched closer. "Did you get collagen injections in your upper lip?"

"I'll never tell." She didn't have to reveal *all* her secrets. The professional she'd visited had assured her the enhancement was completely safe.

"*When* did you do all this?"

"Yesterday. *All* day. It was exhausting. But worth it. I've been enjoying people's reactions this morning."

"Who has seen you? Have the reporters seen you?"

"Yes, but I think they thought someone else spent the night with me, because they're still back at my place waiting for me to come out."

"Oh, that's funny."

"Not really. What if they think I spent the night with another woman?" She wiggled her shapely new eyebrows. "*You know.*"

Bernadine laughed. "That's *really* funny."

Lisa sat on one of the comfortable upholstered chairs.

"They'll figure it out soon." The lawyer gathered a few papers that were stacked on the edge of her desk. "These need signatures."

Lisa picked up a pen. "I hired him."

"Douglas?"

"Yes."

"That's good. We can get the contracts under way for his salary and percentages. I took the liberty of mocking up a couple of standard ones for you to look over."

"Okay. Can I take them to show him? I'm having dinner with him tomorrow night."

"Dinner? Remember what I told you."

"Trust me, I know. He's in this for the money."

"Hon, when we talked about this before you said you hadn't gotten any better looking. Obviously you were good-looking all along, you just weren't letting anyone know. Now… Well, be careful. He's going to be on you like fuzz on a peach."

"I'm a big girl."

"I hope so."

The reporters were smarter than Lisa had given them credit for. They'd figured it out. They followed her home with cameras rolling. This time she turned and waved, did a little runway turn for them and took a bow.

The local evening news showed her in her casual suit and sexy shoes. Even Lisa couldn't believe this Lisa on film was the same person they'd been following. She looked so good. So definitely not a wallflower. Once home she changed, fed the dogs and took them for a run. As daylight waned, she stared into the refrigerator and settled for a bowl of cereal.

She appeared new and different. But she was still the same boring person she'd been all along. She looked a hundred percent better, but she hadn't *changed*. Change on the outside was good, but a metamorphosis had to come from within to be a true difference.

Maybe she was fine just the way she was. She'd been happy with her life before, even with its simplicity. Dogs weren't complicated, and she didn't have to impress anyone. There *was* no one to impress, she thought glumly.

Lisa selected a video, started it and settled on the couch with a bowl of popcorn. Piper and Joey snuggled up on either side and ate an occasional stray kernel. She could change. She could be really exciting if she put her mind to it. And at long last she *did* have someone to impress.

Somewhere around eleven she fell asleep, and Piper ate the rest of the popcorn.

The following evening Riley pulled into the long, narrow drive with a hedge alongside and got out of his red Jaguar. It wasn't dark yet, so the cameras had a good view of him approaching the porch and walking up to Lisa's door. He knocked, and dogs barked immediately.

He could see the massive form of a canine through the lace curtain on the full-length leaded-glass door.

"Get back," Lisa said from inside.

Had she been talking to him? He took a hesitant step back.

The lock turned and she opened the door.

An enormous golden retriever growled menacingly while another barked.

"Joey. Piper. Hush." He thought the woman who spoke to the disturbed animals was Lisa, but he was torn between gaping at her and keeping both eyes on the dogs.

Couldn't do it.

She was wearing a red dress that had a slit clear up one thigh and exposed both her shoulders. The garment fit her sexy, slender body as if it had been made for her, and the shock of knowing she *had* a sexy, slender body hit him full force.

"I'll need to touch you," she said.

He stared at her and fought the physical reaction her words nearly launched. Dark hair with golden highlights framed her face—and what a face it was. Sable arched brows, full shiny lips, eyes as blue and deep as a summer sky. "Lisa?"

"They need to see you're not an intruder." She took his hand and pulled him inside. Standing close beside him, she said, "Put your arm around me."

Riley did as told, draping an arm around her shoulder, his fingers grazing her bare upper arm. She smelled so good, he closed his eyes and *experienced* the feminine scent.

"See, he's a friend," she said. "Let them smell you."

Riley opened his eyes and took his hand away from Lisa to extend it hesitantly toward the dogs. "You're sure?"

She nodded.

The darker-colored of the two padded right up and sniffed the proffered hand, gave it a lick, then sat and panted. The blond retriever kept his distance and growled.

Lisa looked up at Riley and shrugged. "I've never known him to do that. That's Piper. This one's Joey. You boys be good."

She turned the lock and pulled the door shut behind her. Riley watched every stimulating movement.

"You changed your hair." And your body and face and everything else. "And that dress—wow."

"Thanks."

He hurried to open the car door. A smooth length of thigh was exposed when she sat. She adjusted her dress, and he closed the car door and cautioned himself.

It was probably bad manners to ask what she'd done to achieve this incredible new look, but he couldn't get past the fact that she looked nothing like the woman his father had taken to calling "frumpy" and "bohemian." Riley got behind the wheel and concentrated on starting the car and backing up when what he wanted to do was turn and soak her in.

The fact that *that* body had been underneath those awful skirts and jackets all along loosened a screw in his steely confidence. He wasn't used to being so unprepared.

And he'd definitely been unprepared to see her looking like this. Even less prepared to have a very noncerebral reaction.

"Sorry about the rude welcome."

His brain switched tracks and he was glad for the distraction. He couldn't afford to lose his edge. "That's all right."

"The boys are usually very friendly."

"I'm sure they are."

"They're protective of me."

"Sure." He pulled out onto the highway and headed toward Billings. "Lisa, you look incredible."

"Thanks."

"No, I mean, you look *incredible*. What… I mean, what…?"

"Don't say it. I was ready for a change and I did it, that's all."

"You're...beautiful."

She was too quiet and he knew he'd said the wrong thing at the wrong time, no matter how true it was. He glanced over to see her looking out the passenger window. She raised her chin a little, turned to face him and smiled hesitantly.

A beautiful smile, too. Familiar and yet so different. "Want some music?"

She glanced the dashboard. "Sure."

He flipped open the console between them. "Pick something."

A silver bracelet dangled on her wrist as she reached to look through the CDs. She flipped through The Flaming Lips, B.B. King and The Doobie Brothers to hand him one by Norah Jones. He gave her a sideways glance but placed the disc in the tray and pushed Play. Was there any meaning behind her selection?

The strains of a sultry song filled the interior of the car. Surely she didn't intend to seduce him. Or to be seductive. Riley tried to think of something to say to her that wasn't about how good she looked. Not much else entered his mind at the moment. "So, you like dogs?"

"Yes," she replied easily. "They're not as judgmental or as critical as people."

"Can't take one to a movie."

"My dogs watch movies with me all the time."

"Can't teach one to play chess."

"I don't play chess either, so that's never been a compatibility issue."

"So, in your opinion a dog is as good a companion as a person?"

"More so." She glanced at him and her forehead furrowed. "You don't like dogs?"

"I like dogs. At least, the respectable ones."

"Respectable?"

"Some breeds you just can't respect."

"What are you talking about?"

"My mother has the most foolish-looking poodle. It's four feet tall and its fur is cut into ridiculous pom-poms."

"Derek," she said.

"Oh, you know Derek. Then you can see how I just can't respect that dog."

"He's friendly and very smart. Well behaved, too. I've taken care of him a few times."

Riley shook his head in distaste.

"There, you see? You're judging him by his looks."

"Well…yeah."

"He can't help how he looks. It's his breed. And the way your mother has him cut."

He wasn't earning any points with this conversation. She was starting to take his comments personally. "Sorry. You're probably right."

She glanced at him. "What about horses?"

"What do you mean?"

"Do they have to be perfect in order for you to respect them?"

"Horses demand respect."

"How so? Their size? Because they're not as intelligent as dogs."

Riley held up a hand in frustration. "I'm sorry I brought up Derek, okay? I'll try to adjust my attitude."

"Just because I said something?"

"Yes."

She smoothed her skirt over her knees. "I won't even ask about your attitude toward women."

"Thank you."

She laughed softly, and he understood she was having fun at his expense. He wasn't used to his comments and opinions being taken lightly or challenged. This evening wasn't going in the direction he'd planned. Well, maybe the direction was okay, but the person in the metaphorical driver's seat was in question. He needed to keep things where he wanted them.

"My mother's planning a reception to celebrate the ground-breaking for the resort," he told her.

"I guess the ski resort is a pretty big deal, huh?"

"It is. It will bring tourists to Thunder Canyon for more than the summer months. Right now we rely heavily on Heritage Days and the cabins and trail rides, but all that's seasonal. This will bring in more revenue."

"I have a few pet owners in the new homes out north. New Town is expanding."

She hadn't even picked up on his lead. "The reason I brought it up was to ask you to attend the reception."

Lisa glanced over at him in surprise. "I really don't think I'd fit in."

"Your status is changing. You own property, significant property. And very soon, once that mine is producing, you'll be investing. As your manager, I'm going to suggest strongly that you invest a percent locally. Public relations is an important part of business."

"So you think I should attend the reception for PR purposes?"

"Partially."

She didn't ask what the other part was. Was he pushing her a little too firmly?

"All right," she said, surprising him. "When is it?"

He told her the time and date and they made arrangements.

A few minutes later they reached Billings and he drove to the restaurant where he'd made reservations.

When they'd gone to the mine, Lisa had opened her own door before he could get around, but this time she waited. He walked beside her to the building and held the door.

A hostess showed them to their table and brought menus.

Lisa's eyebrows rose as she studied the menu. She glanced hesitantly at their neighboring tables.

"Something wrong?" Riley asked.

"It's so expensive," she whispered.

"It's okay," he replied in the same hushed tone. "I'm good for it."

When the waiter came, Lisa ordered a steak with a baked potato and Riley asked for the same. He couldn't remember the last time he'd been with a woman who'd ordered a regular meal and not a salad or seafood.

"Have you looked over the wine selection?" the waiter asked.

"Would you drink wine if I ordered it?" Riley asked her.

"Will you cut me off before my face goes numb?"

With a grin he picked up the list and held it so they could both read it. "I'll make sure of it."

Something about the way she studied the list, running her finger down the columns, struck him as familiar, but he couldn't figure out why. They'd never done this before, never eaten out or read a wine list together. He shrugged off the feeling of déjà vu.

"Let's get this out of the way," she said and took several papers from her bag and unfolded them. "These are agreements my lawyer drew up for our working arrangement."

He read them over quickly. "She faxed me copies so I could read them ahead of time. Got a pen?"

He signed them with a flourish, and Lisa tucked them back into her bag.

"Well, that's official," she said, not sure whether to be pleased or panicky. He was working for her. Maybe it would seem real once she'd seen some gold.

The deep red Merlot Riley had ordered arrived, and the waiter poured a dollop in a glass for him to taste. It was dry and rich, an excellent blend of flavors.

After it was poured, Lisa tasted hers.

"Impressed?" he asked.

"I'm impressed by anything without a screw-on cap. How do you know which wine to order?"

"I've toured several wineries and I belong to an international club. I subscribe to a couple of publications. You learn the same way you learn anything else."

"Only if you can afford to try the really good stuff," she added.

He nodded in concession to her point. He didn't suppose dog walking afforded her the luxury to purchase vintage wines.

"I'm trying not to think inside the same parameters," she told him. "Small, I mean. Cheap. But my bank account hasn't actually caught up yet, so it's not easy to break away from the habits."

"I've given some thought to that problem." He set his glass down. "You have to have money to make money— it's that simple. There are expenses in getting the mining under way. People must be hired and fees paid and there are all number of things cropping up. In the old days, a miner got a grubstake."

"Someone gave him money for his supplies with the understanding that it would be paid back once the strike came in," she replied.

Riley nodded. "Yes. The Queen of Hearts is a sure thing. It's not even a risk. You have gold sitting there waiting to be extracted. I'd like to grubstake the expenses for you. Give you a substantial amount to get you started and tide you over until the mining is well under way. It should be less than a month before that happens."

"I can wait," she said easily and watched as the waiter came by and filled their glasses.

"But you don't have to wait," Riley continued once the man had gone. "You could have money for the things you need now. I've seen that bucket of bolts you drive. You need a better car."

She glanced aside, but he could tell she was thinking.

"All the meetings are taking you away from your regular job, so there's a dent in that income, right?"

She sipped her wine and said lightly, "No, I'm juggling time for my pets."

"You can think about it."

"I don't need to think about it. I already owe you for security and safety measures and who knows what all, I don't want to owe you for personal items, as well."

"It wouldn't be that much, Lisa."

"Not that much? A new car? Excuse me, a new car is much."

"Comparatively speaking. It won't be that much compared to how much you'll be generating from the mine."

"And I can wait. I don't like the idea of being in debt."

She hadn't added the words *to you,* but they were there just the same. He raised a hand to say he was finished talking about the advance. He'd made the offer. If she was too stubborn to see the practicality of it, that was her problem.

He changed the subject to advice on how to deal with the people she'd be working with from now on. As the meal was delivered, he poured them both more wine. It was obvious she enjoyed it. Turning their attention to the food and the conversation, the tension between them eased.

"Body language is an important part of communication in business," he told her. "And there are ways to gain an advantage."

"Okay, what are they?"

"To dominate another, take control of their time. Make them wait for you."

"Isn't that rude?"

"No, it's controlling an encounter."

"What if the other person tries to make me wait?"

"Counter it. Make him wait for you. And always

choose where and how you sit. Don't take a low chair, and if there's no choice, sit on the edge or stand."

Lisa cut a bite of her steak and asked, "They taught you this stuff in business college?"

A flash went off before he could reply, and Riley glanced over his shoulder to see a man with a camera just inside the room.

Lisa set down her fork and dabbed her lips with her napkin. She waved pleasantly and raised her glass of wine toward the intruder. "Did you get the label on our wine bottle clearly?" she called. "Because it's a very good vintage. I could turn it a little bit."

Riley glanced from her to the reporter, who was joined now by two others. The other restaurant patrons were staring.

He leaned forward. "Don't you have a restraining order?"

"Yes."

He reached inside his jacket and pulled out his phone. "Then I'm calling the police."

Lisa pointed to Riley's phone but looked toward the reporters. "He's calling the police," she called. "You might want to move on."

His call was answered and he gave the dispatcher the details.

"This is Miss Martin's restraining order," the officer said. "She needs to make the complaint."

He extended the phone. "You have to report it."

She accepted it without hesitation. "Hi," she said. "The paparazzi are interrupting my dinner. Could you speak with them? I think they'll go if you just talk to them."

She got out of her seat to walk across the room.

More flashes popped, but she walked directly up to the nearest man with a camera. "It's for you," she said. "The police."

Chapter Six

Riley stood and followed a few feet behind her. He
watched the bizarre scene unfold and couldn't help
glancing at the curiously staring diners. The reporters
looked more uncomfortable at being called out than
Lisa did at confronting them. No matter how unortho-
dox her method, she'd deftly turned the tables and had
the situation firmly in control. Maybe she didn't need
his advice as much as he'd first thought.

"Go ahead," she said to the officer on the phone.
"I'm putting the offender on now." She pointed to
Riley's cell phone and handed it to the man whose camera was now lowered. The other two men first zeroed in
for close-ups of the newly transformed heiress, then
trained their lenses on the one-sided phone conversation.

"Hello?" the man said uncertainly. "Er, yes. Chad Falkner. Uh-huh. Yes, I'm aware. Certainly. All right. Now, yes. Er, thanks."

He handed the phone back to Lisa and turned to the men beside him. "We're outta here or they're coming to arrest us."

"I knew you'd see reason," she told them, still speaking in a friendly manner. "Hey, none of us wants to be made a spectacle of, do we?" She put the phone to her ear. "Thanks, Officer. They'll be going now."

She flipped the phone shut and extended it to Riley.

He stifled the urge to laugh while he tucked it away, and a sudden idea occurred. He stepped forward. "Excuse me, but may I make a suggestion?"

The restaurant manager hurried toward them at that moment, a concerned look on his face. "Is there a problem? Would you like to use my office? Or perhaps your party could step outside so as not to disturb the other diners."

"Did you get *this* on film?" Lisa asked the young man who still aimed a camera.

"I did," he said.

"How about him?" she asked, indicating the reporter who'd spoken with the police and was clearly at a loss for what to say or do next. "Did you get him talking to the police?"

The same reporter nodded.

"Let's step outside for a minute," Riley said, finally taking control.

He and Lisa and the manager accompanied the three reporters out the door. They stood on the pavement in front of the building. Night had fallen and insects buzzed around the neon signs that lit their small gathering.

"I'd like to make a proposition," Riley began. "And Miss Martin, you call me out if this is out of line or if you don't agree. I suggest Miss Martin give you an exclusive personal interview—"

"Wait a minute," Lisa started to object.

"Let me finish," he insisted and turned back to the reporters. "An exclusive personal interview at a time and place of her choosing and at her discretion. Taped, not live. You will provide her with the questions ahead of time. She can refuse to answer any she wishes, and she'll be allowed to provide questions she wants to be asked. She'll have the right to preview the interview before it's aired.

"In return for this gracious gift of her time and the sacrifice of privacy, you will leave her alone for an entire week following the airing." He faced Lisa. "Miss Martin, how do you feel about this?"

She glanced from Riley to the reporters and replied without hesitation. "Sure."

"And you, gentlemen?"

The media people all needed permission from their superiors, but all three were eager for the opportunity. Riley took their names and numbers and gave them his business card in return. Chad Falkner smirked as though he'd been granted an interview with Julia Roberts.

"Now if you'll excuse us," Riley said, "we have a dinner to finish."

When they returned to their table, their plates were missing. "I had your meals kept warm for you, sir," their waiter said. He signaled, and a moment later their dinners were returned.

Lisa's hesitant glance took in patrons at other tables, then raised to his.

"That was the last thing I expected you to do," he told her. "Confronting them like that. You were great."

"I'm all about your pleasure," she said, picking up her fork.

The double meaning of that statement zapped other coherent thought from his head. She wasn't anything he'd expected her to be, nothing like the reticent young woman he'd planned to befriend and assist. "You keep surprising me," he said honestly.

"I'm surprising myself."

He studied her features, her shiny hair and the way the light glowed on her bare shoulders. He wasn't the one who was supposed to feel as if he was walking on marbles. He had to be very careful around this woman.

"I've begun asking myself what Lily would have done."

"Lily Divine?"

"My great-great-grandmother. I think there's a lot more we don't know about her. And a lot we think we know that isn't true."

"Like what?"

"She's famous for being the Shady Lady, but that was just the name of her saloon. I don't think she was a prostitute."

"How do you explain that painting over the bar?"

"I don't know. I don't know that I have to."

"The dresses? The saloon?"

She looked him in the eye. "You can hang fuzzy dice

around your neck and go stand in your garage, but that doesn't make you a car."

He laughed.

She laid down her fork and placed her napkin on the table. "I've been reading your great-great-grandmother's journals."

"Which grandmother?"

"Catherine Douglas. Amos's wife."

"I've never heard about any journals."

"Well, they belong to Tildy Matheson now. Remember you told me about Emily Stanton and Brad Vaughn going through things at Tildy's and finding the deed? Well, it seems Catherine left her belongings to Tildy's grandmother."

"That's strange."

"She plans to bequeath a trunk full of items to the historical society."

"It's odd those things weren't kept in the family," he said, thinking out loud.

"Many families don't have heirlooms because things get discarded before they're actually valuable or have much sentiment. It's fortunate that someone kept these things in good condition."

He could see that and nodded his agreement.

She picked up her glass and sipped wine. The recessed lighting flattered her dark hair and the sparkle in her eyes accentuated the feminine hollows of her collarbone and the curve of her shoulders. Riley noticed the way the red fabric was designed to loop over the top of each arm and drape suggestively across her breasts.

He didn't remember much about the painting of the

Shady Lady except those exceptionally appealing breasts. At some time or another, he'd bet every teenage boy in Thunder Canyon had been intrigued by that enigmatic woman from the town's past…and by her breasts. In the next heartbeat his thoughts took a natural turn and he imagined Lisa without the dress. The mental image was a complete turn-on.

"Would you like to see them?"

If he'd been standing, he would have fallen. *Here?* She was looking into his face, and he made himself meet her eyes. His heart pounded.

"Riley, would you like to see the journals?"

"Oh! Yes. I'd love to see the journals…thanks."

"If you don't have any other plans, you can come to my place when we've finished eating. What kind of business do we need to discuss?"

He gathered his senses. "State and federal regulators. Water-quality inspectors. Ladders and escape routes."

"You really know about all that stuff?"

"I'm educating myself on the aspects of mining so I can advise you."

"That's as impressive as the wine."

He filled her in on what the inspectors would be looking for the next day. "The rest can wait," he told her. "We've talked enough business this evening."

She smiled. "I agree."

Lisa'd had him figured out since day one. She took a swallow of the luscious wine and let the warm glow suffuse her insides and spread to her limbs. He'd been hell-bent on endearing himself to her, making his services indispensable, and truth be told, she didn't mind all that much. She needed the know-how, experience and quick mind he had to offer. She didn't mind the attention. But his ruse was so transparent, she'd have to be blindfolded in a dark, windowless room not to see it.

His surprise at her transformation was gratifying. More than gratifying. *Delicious.* She'd caught him off guard. Turned the tables on Mr. Cool. She was sure he'd intended to impress her with an expensive meal and this incredible wine and his charming company. But he'd been expecting to impress and win over the Lisa with the baggy clothing and the wild coils of hair, not this new and improved version.

She smiled to herself. Maybe he'd just have to try a little harder now. Seeing him give his all could prove… rewarding.

"What's so amusing?" he asked.

"Nothing."

He raised one ebony eyebrow in question.

"A girl can have her secrets, can't she?" She chuckled at that because it sounded so ridiculous to her own ears. But her pathetic attempt at flirting must have been pretty good because he smiled, too, and his gaze traveled her face and hair in an altogether appreciative and intriguing way.

Lisa had been determined to break out of her timid, boring self and become someone confident and exciting. So far so good. She had him fooled, anyway.

What would someone named Lily Divine do if she was finally given the chance to stir things up with a man she'd had the hots for since adolescence? Okay, not the hots necessarily. Back then it had been an innocent unrequited yearning. *Now* it was the hots.

Well, someone confident like Lily would probably cast inhibition to the wind and grab opportunity with both fists. "Do you want dessert?" she asked.

"Do you?"

"I have brownies, ice cream and fudge topping at my place."

A grin tilted his lips, drawing her attention to their shape. "More wine?"

The bottle was empty. She wanted to remember the rest of the evening. "Better not. I can't feel my nose."

He signaled to their waiter, signed for the check and accompanied her to the door.

It was full dark now, a luminous crescent moon bright in the summer sky. Riley placed his hand in the small of her back as they walked toward the car. The warmth of his touch suffused the fabric of her dress and ignited another glow inside her.

They reached the red Jaguar, and Lisa heard the whir of a camera. Riley had opened her door and she turned to face him, standing in the minimal space between his body and the interior. "Maybe my place isn't such a good idea," she said, and her disappointment was sincere. "I have to think about tomorrow's headlines."

"What about the ice cream? And the journals?" he asked.

She shrugged.

"I can lose those guys. And I know of someplace private."

"Where?"

He leaned close so he couldn't possibly be overheard. "I have a cabin outside town. No one except family knows about it."

His whisper created goose bumps down her arms and across her shoulders. She looked up at him in the moonlight. "Then you'd better go back in and order dessert to go."

A grin spread across his face and he ushered her onto the seat. He was only gone a few minutes. She'd seen the way the staff catered to him. They'd probably run for the dessert.

"What is it?" she asked.

"Chocolate-raspberry truffle sound all right?"

She groaned. Chocolate bribes were a no-fail tactic with a woman like her.

He chuckled and started the car.

Within minutes he'd led the news vans away from town and was driving north on Thunder Canyon Road. He sped up, signaled as though he was turning toward his ranch, then quickly turned off the headlights and traveled straight ahead.

"How can you see?" she asked.

"I know where I'm going."

"You'd better tell me you can see. This is making me nervous."

"Just a little farther and I'll turn the lights back on." He approached a row of trees, which must have been what he was looking for, turned onto a side road and stopped. He turned off the engine and got out.

"Where are you going?"

"I'm checking to make sure no one is following us."

She had known him in high school. His family had

been respected—as well as resented—in this town for over a hundred years. She didn't think there'd been any serial killers in the Douglas line, but she probably should have checked before coming out in the wilderness with him.

He walked behind the car and returned after a few minutes. "Okay, we lost them."

After turning the headlights back on, he drove back onto the road, traveled what she thought was north for another twenty or thirty minutes, then took a left turn and headed along a dirt road lined with trees and tall grass. A deer sprang out of the foliage, and Riley braked until the animal bounded from sight.

Lisa was lost now, couldn't have found her way back alone, and she'd seen too many movies to not have a twinge of discomfort at her predicament. "Where are we?"

"Northwest of our ranch."

Finally he drove into a clearing where a well and a couple of shingle-sided outbuildings stood. He pulled directly in front of double doors, then got out to open them, and Lisa peered into the garage-like structure. He drove in, turned off the engine and grabbed the carry-out bag.

After locking the place, he led her up a lighted stairway.

"This is darker than the mine," she said. She seemed willing to let this man take her anywhere. Why was that?

"We'll be upstairs in a minute." He took her hand, and most of her doubts dissolved at the warm, strong touch. Lily wouldn't have had second thoughts about this adventure. Lisa wasn't going to let cold feet put crazy thoughts in her head. At the top was a landing and another door, and he opened it, guiding her into a dark room.

Riley stretched her arm as he groped for something, and a moment later fluorescent lights came on.

Lisa blinked. They stood in a kitchen. A well-appointed kitchen with stainless-steel appliances, wood flooring and a pine table and chairs. The open floor plan revealed a living area with comfortable sofas and chairs and a stone fireplace. Probably not someplace a serial killer would take his victims. Besides, dozens of people had seen them together tonight and even more would see their pictures tomorrow. "*This* is your *cabin?*"

"It's made of logs."

So it was. "How can it be that no one knows this place is here? Who built it? And delivered the furniture?"

"I hired an out-of-state builder. Brought the furnishings in myself."

"The appliances, too?"

"Remember me mentioning my financial advisor, Phil Wagner?"

"Yes."

"He's a friend. He helped. He uses the place whenever he wants."

Money will buy just about anything, she thought to herself. Even respectability. Anonymity. "If I asked you to take me home right this minute, what would you say?"

"Before dessert?"

She grinned. She'd had to double-check, after all. "You have newfangled plumbing in this rustic place?"

"There's a tiny bathroom in that hall right there, another bath through a suite of rooms you'll see on your left."

Size didn't matter right this moment. She found the closest functional room and minutes later felt much better. In the maple-framed mirror Lisa studied a reflection she wasn't used to confronting yet. Just seeing her new self reinforced her confidence. No wonder Riley looked at her differently. No wonder she felt so different. The new and improved Lisa was a force to be reckoned with. A chick with a life.

All the hard work that had gone into straightening her hair, selecting her clothing and putting together her new look had been worth the time and effort.

She wasn't sitting home sharing snacks with her dogs tonight. As soon as that thought surfaced, she experienced a twinge of guilt. *Sorry, boys.* She really liked those nights, too. But tonight was her night to shine. Riley was sniffing out more than popcorn, and she was liking it.

Returning to the other room, she discovered Riley had softened the lighting and made coffee. Chocolate-raspberry truffle waited on two small white plates.

"I have a sauvignon dessert wine if you'd prefer," he offered.

"No, the coffee smells really good."

"Have a seat and I'll pour us each a cup."

He brought two mugs of steaming coffee and sat them on the low table.

Lisa savored her dessert, momentarily closing her eyes and indulging. "This is incredible. Have you had it before?"

"No." He observed her with a mixture of awe and uncertainty that she took pleasure in knowing she inspired.

One of the reasons she didn't want to drink any more was that she already felt as if she was watching a bold new Lisa living her life. It was an odd feeling, but the impression was liberating. The times, they were a-changin', and she had to catch up with them.

"So," she said to break the silence that had stretched. "Only your family knows about this place."

"And Phil."

"And your friend, Phil. Does your family drop by? Use the cabin?"

He finished the bite he'd taken. "No, none of them drop by. Or use the cabin."

"How big is your family?" She didn't recall him having any brothers or sisters.

"My mom's from a large family, so I have a lot of aunts and uncles. When they visit my mom, they stay at the big house at the ranch. I have an adopted sister, Katie."

"Are you close to her?"

"Always was. She married at the first of the year."

Lisa heard something peculiar in Riley's tone when he spoke of his adopted sister's marriage. "Do I sense some tension there?"

"You didn't read about Katie and Justin Caldwell? Or see them on the news?"

"You mean Katie Fenton, the librarian? I know her from the library, and yes, I read about her playing the mail-order bride in this year's Heritage Day celebration. Someone stepped in to play the groom because Ben Saunders was sick. Some big-business type from out of town. They got snowed in together at the museum."

"That was Justin."

"Oh."

"Come to find out Justin was in town to get back at my father for using and discarding his mother—and then turning his back on Justin."

Lisa didn't understand his meaning, so she waited for Riley to explain, if he was going to. Her brain was probably still a little dulled from the wine.

"Seems my mother had a difficult time when I was born. She found out she couldn't have more children and she got depressed. She was too disturbed to properly care for me. And she turned my father away. He in turn took his interest elsewhere and got Justin's mother pregnant."

"Oh." She was sure that wasn't an insightful response, but his disclosure caught her by surprise. "So… Justin Caldwell is your brother."

"Half," he clarified. "He undermined us with the investors we had secured for the ski resort and took control away from my father. Then he told him who he was and why he'd done it."

"That was deceitful."

"He thought he had his reasons."

"You're defending him?"

"No. He did that as retribution for things he felt were done wrong against himself and his mother. It was a terrible time for my father—and for my mother when she learned the truth. Our family suffered because of it."

"I'm sure there wouldn't have been a good way for you and your mother to find out."

"You're right about that."

"Adele is a lovely woman and she's always been very

kind to me. That's more than I can say for a lot of people in this town."

"My father locked himself in his study and wouldn't talk to me or my mother. It was only Katie he allowed in, and she's the one he told the whole sordid story to."

The hurt in that disclosure was obvious.

"He had given Justin's mother half a million dollars so that he could keep the baby. But she took Justin and the money and disappeared. Caleb wanted Justin to know he wanted him and asked Katie to get him to listen."

"The whole thing must have been awful for you," she said.

He shrugged as though it was of little consequence. "I give Justin credit for doing right in the end. When he learned that my father did care, he ended up turning control of the ski resort back over."

"So the two of you are on good terms?"

"We're okay."

"What about Justin and your father?"

"Hell, they're golf buddies."

"And your mother?"

"She's accepted Justin. His birth wasn't his fault."

"Neither was yours."

He looked aside at that remark. "I've never talked about this before."

She could understand why. "You managed to keep most of this out of the news, obviously. I don't remember reading anything about it."

"No one really knew what went on, and my father certainly didn't want the truth made public. He gave enough information to satisfy them and not enough to paint himself in a bad light."

"But he's recognized Justin as his son?"

"Yes. 'From a previous marriage' was the slant the papers got when the story finally broke."

"But he's not older than you."

"He wasn't born here, and since no one doubted the truth, the facts weren't checked. Suits the Douglas family."

Lisa sipped the dark brew. "This is incredible coffee."

"It's a blend Marge orders for me." He stood and removed his jacket. "Want to take another cup and sit outdoors? The porch is pretty high above the foliage, so it's usually free of mosquitoes."

The porch extended along two sides of the cabin and was furnished with comfortably padded chairs and chaise lounges. The half moon offered a silvered view of treetops and dark distant mountains. Fireflies dotted the landscape and frogs chirped. Lisa stood at the railing and gazed out into the darkness. The seclusion and cocooning silence lent a sense of peace to what had been unusually crazy days.

"It's a fantastic view in the daylight," he said.

"I'll bet the boys would love it here. They'd chase squirrels and rabbits to their hearts' content."

"You're welcome to use the place anytime. Bring them and hide out if you like."

"I'd never be able to find it."

"I'd show you." His voice came from right behind her. "Think about it."

"You're always giving me things to think about."

"I have good ideas."

She turned to find him studying her. The light from the front windows illuminated his features. Her heart fluttered unexpectedly. Just nerves, she thought to herself.

Lisa could count on one hand the number of dates she'd had in her life. Each one had been awkward and the conversation had been stilted, and she felt exactly the same way now as she had on those occasions: out of place. Was this a date? What did couples say to each other?

Her heart sped up. What did more-than-dating couples say to each other? She couldn't imagine. She'd watched a hundred movies in which the man and woman flirted and talked and ended up in bed together, but movies were fantasy, and though she loved those cinematic escapes, she was grounded firmly in reality.

What would Meg Ryan say to Tom Hanks right now? What would Kathleen Turner say to Michael Douglas?

"What's your favorite movie?"

He glanced toward the mountains, then back at her. "I don't watch a whole lot of movies."

"You don't?"

"No."

"Why not?"

"I don't know. Just don't take time."

"But you've seen movies."

"Of course."

"Then what's your favorite from those you've seen?"

He shrugged, seeming almost uncomfortable at being asked.

"What came to mind when I asked?"

"*Platoon.*"

Lisa resisted wrinkling her nose. She hated war movies.

"What's your favorite movie?" he asked.

"I have a lot of favorites. A whole case of them, as a matter of fact."

"You made me pick one."

"Okay," she conceded. *"Roman Holiday."*

"Audrey Hepburn?"

She nodded. "And Gregory Peck."

"What's so appealing about it?"

She thought it over. "The heroine escapes her real life and has an adventure with no one knowing her true identity."

"I see the appeal."

"You do? Have you ever thought you'd like to be someone else for a while?"

"Not really."

"Too practical to have fantasies like that, huh?"

He touched her bare arm and a shiver darted up her spine. "Nothing wrong with fantasies," he said.

Lisa closed her eyes and heard the thump of her heart. Felt the chug of her blood in her veins and the heat of his hand on her arm. What would Lily say now?

He ran his palm up her arm, found her collarbone with one finger and stroked it.

Lily probably wouldn't waste time talking. Or even thinking.

Lisa opened her eyes and deliberately stepped into Riley's arms.

Chapter Seven

Lisa had never known there were kisses like this outside the movies. His lips on hers awakened a need that had been dormant inside her for a long, long time. It was easy to press uncertainty aside and lose herself in the sensations. He was warm. And strong. But she didn't delude herself that he felt anything for her. She wouldn't even let herself wonder if he felt the same flooding warmth and physical hunger she did at this moment, because she didn't want to spoil her fantasy come true.

Riley parted her lips and curled his tongue against hers in a deep, mind-drugging foray. Lisa slid her hands up along the hard, warm plane of his shirt front, wrapped her arms around his neck and pressed her body against his.

This evening, this moment, in Riley's arms she felt desirable for the first time. She wanted to sink all the way into this experience, to finally know passion and feel good about herself.

With one palm she framed his jaw. The unfamiliar texture of his cheek sent a jolt of excitement through her nerve endings. He turned into her touch and kissed her palm, his mouth hot and wet and more erotic than anything she'd ever known.

With both hands she bracketed his face and pulled his mouth back to hers for another staggering kiss.

Riley flattened one hand on her spine. With the other he rubbed her shoulder blade, stroked her bare arm and then cupped her breast. Her nipples were taut and her body thrummed with tense awareness. She wished she wasn't wearing this bra. Lisa felt exhilarated and sluggish at the same time and she didn't know how long she could stand on her own.

Maybe she gave him some sign of her lack of stamina, because he moved them both so that her back was against a wooden pillar. By insinuating one knee between her thighs, he prevented her from slipping to the floor but at the same time created a new and more disturbing sensation.

With both hands free he explored the contours of her body through her dress and caressed her breasts as best he could above her body shaper, soothing one ache while he created another. "You're incredible, Lisa," he whispered. "So beautiful."

His words were potent, giving her confidence, empowering her. She had planned this, she thought with smug satisfaction. Orchestrated events to her liking. And it wasn't over yet. Plain Lisa Jane Martin had Riley Douglas right where she wanted him.

Well…*almost.*

With renewed strength she left his lips and straightened to the task of loosening his tie. When he reached to assist, she pushed his hand away and tugged it off herself, then unbuttoned his shirt. Underneath he wore a stark white T-shirt that almost glowed in the moonlight. She ran her hands over his chest through the soft fabric, and he eased back only enough to tug it off over his head.

She let her fingers hover over his skin for a moment, anticipating the warmth of his flesh. She heard his intake of breath and looked up to read expectancy and arousal on his shadowed face. Lisa's heart pounded with anticipation.

She touched his chest then, soft hair, warm skin, lean muscle beneath. With his hands at her hips he simply experienced her exploratory caress.

Senses filled to brimming with his textures and heat, she ran a finger over his lips, then leaned upward for more kisses.

As he obliged her, Riley found the zipper on the back of her dress and pulled it down, lowering the front.

The salesgirl had told her the black strapless corset was all the rage. Putting it on, Lisa had compared it to a sausage casing, but the end result had made the dress fit perfectly. Riley *was* looking at her as if she were a mouthwatering breakfast, and she didn't mind.

He took the support of his knee away, so that she had to stand on her own, and he leaned down to kiss the tops of her breasts where they spilled over the corset. The tingling sensation his lips created sent Lisa's blood pulsing.

He straightened and kissed her again.

What was expected now? What was she supposed to say? Or do? She refused to show her awkwardness about any of this. Would he ask her if she wanted to get comfortable? Would he invite her into his bedroom? That might ruin the spontaneity, but she couldn't quite see baring it all out here on the porch with a thirty-foot drop below.

The thought gave her a twinge of panic. "Can we go inside?"

"Sure." He took her hand and she held up the front of her dress as he led her easily into the house. He paused and looked into her eyes. "Upstairs?"

One word, but it was his way of asking if they were going to move forward with what they'd started, as well as her chance to call a halt if she chose.

The same word gave him her answer. "Upstairs."

He let her walk ahead of him up a winding black wrought-iron staircase. From behind he finished unzipping her dress and cupped her bottom as though he couldn't keep his hands off her.

At the top he pointed to an open doorway, and she preceded him into the bedroom. After turning on a bathroom light, he left the door open a sliver, permitting only a slim measure of light to escape.

His broad form was in silhouette as he came toward her. Lisa's heart thudded with swift and unexpected delight and she kicked off her shoes. She'd imagined moments like this a hundred times in her girlish fantasies, and now her dreams had come to life. Riley leaned over the bed and, with a swoosh of silken fabric, pulled back a dark coverlet.

She let her dress fall to the floor and stepped out of it. There wasn't a second left for awkwardness, because he reached for her and snagged her around the waist, pulling her down with him on the bed. The sheets were cool against her bare back. Satin.

"This is sexy, but let's get rid of it," he said, reaching to find the hooks on her corset. *Good luck,* she thought, but he found the fasteners and released her breasts from their confinement.

He definitely knew what he was doing when he found her hard, sensitive nipple with his tongue. Freedom was one thing, but indulgence, oh, indulgence was even better, she discovered with a shudder. *This* was what she'd been missing. *This* was what scriptwriters tried to convey on screen and novel writers attempted to put on paper. No one had ever described it well enough.

She had a lot to learn.

Riley lavished attention on each breast and then on her mouth again. She wasn't sure which one of them reached for her underwear, but they both gave a tug from a different angle and the cotton garment was tossed aside. Gwen had tried to talk Lisa into a thong, but French-cut briefs had been as far as she'd been comfortable going. At this point she didn't think Riley would have noticed or cared if she'd been wearing boxers.

And surprisingly the complete lack of clothing didn't matter to her. She'd shrugged off her inhibitions the moment she'd put on the red dress.

This woman made Riley so hot, he didn't know how he was going to last long enough to perform the act. She'd been turning the tables on him for days. Tonight she had turned him inside out. Showing up in that dress and with that look in her eyes—that look that dared him to try not to fall victim to her seductiveness.

He dipped his hand lower and found her slick and swollen.

She made a sound halfway between a laugh and a cry.

He kissed her again because nothing was enough. Her mouth was sweet and her reactions so artlessly real, he'd lost himself in their first kiss and didn't want to be found.

She set his senses ablaze. "Your skin is so smooth," he praised her.

She bracketed his face with both hands, as though intent on his words.

"Your breasts…"

"What about them?"

They were gorgeous. Full and sensitive. "Let me just say…Lily Divine passed on some incredible genes."

Her lazy smile tipped his equilibrium.

When had he lost control of this game?

When had Lisa Martin become someone he *desired?*

He didn't want to think about it. He shucked out of the rest of his clothing and took great care in kissing and stroking her, tasting the skin behind her ears and at her throat. He used his fingers to coax a series of surprised little gasps and had her raising her hips off the bed.

She grasped his shoulders so hard, her nails bit into his skin. "Riley," she said breathlessly.

"Yes?" He looked into her eyes in the darkness.

"Nothing. I just wanted to say your name."

"Say it, then."

"Riley Douglas."

He reached for the night table, found the box of condoms he'd placed in the drawer earlier and sheathed himself.

She touched his shoulder almost hesitantly.

Riley leaned over her and kissed her. She drew him down to her, eagerly accommodating his weight.

"Keep kissing me," she urged.

He did and guided himself, hoping he wasn't shaking as much on the outside as he was on the inside.

Lisa sought his tongue and took it into her mouth in an erotic imitation of what their bodies were straining to do.

"Relax, Lisa."

"Riley."

Was she just saying his name again? Entering her took a moment of intense concentration while he kissed her and purposefully eased his way.

Her body accepted him all at once, and she grasped his upper arms at the same moment, as though he'd just pushed past a resistance.

Dull recognition nagged at the back of his mind while extreme pleasure flooded his senses. "Lisa, what…?"

"Don't say anything." She wrapped herself around him and made him forget reason and thought.

All that existed in the moments that followed was the two of them floating on a sensual ocean of enjoyment.

Somewhere in the back of his mind he knew she was taking more from him than he'd ever intended to offer, but he couldn't hold back. He wanted to give her more and he wanted more of her. As though detachment hadn't been bred into him from birth, he wanted all of her. Riley felt as if he'd been missing this, even though they'd never before shared a bed.

She climaxed with a soft groan and a shudder, and he gritted his teeth to draw the pleasure out for her. When her body relaxed, he allowed his own swift release and then shifted his weight to her side and kissed her.

She met his gaze in the darkness, and he thought he sensed a question. He threaded his fingers through her hair, combing it away from her face, and caressed her cheek with a thumb. But she said nothing.

Lisa wrapped her fingers around his wrist and moved so she could lie comfortably and kiss him.

Time didn't exist as their hearts returned to a normal beat and the air-conditioning cooled their heated skin. Riley couldn't remember ever spending leisurely after-sex time with a woman before. He wanted to kiss her as much now as he had hours ago. And he was still enjoying it every bit as much as before they'd had sex.

He'd only had this place a few months, but he'd planned to keep the cabin to himself. He was glad it had been Lisa he'd broken the rules for. He was glad he'd brought her.

He ran his fingers through her hair, catching in the tangles they'd created together. He lowered his face to the crook of her neck and inhaled her scent—a scent more intoxicating than the wine—then placed slow kisses along her shoulder.

They lay with their legs tangled, and she sensuously rubbed the sole of her foot against his calf.

Riley rose over her and looked into her eyes before he kissed her. Within minutes he was ready again and she was smiling a welcome.

Lisa had dozed for a few minutes, but she woke to the unfamiliarity of the room and her bed companion. She had to go to the bathroom, so she got up and closed herself in the adjoining bath. The reality of what she'd done tried to burst her bubble of pleasure, but she fought it. She'd known full well what she was doing. She'd wanted this more than anything. She wasn't going to be sorry now. A minute later she padded out and gathered her clothing.

"I have to go home. The boys will need to go out."

Riley leaned on one elbow. "Can't they wait till morning?"

"I never leave them alone this long at night." She took her clothes into the bathroom and talked to him through the partially open door as she dressed. "Besides, we don't want to be seen returning to my place in the morning."

"You're right." The sound of sheets rustling accompanied a click as he turned on a lamp. She saw the light through the crack in the doorway as she stuffed herself into the corset.

"My God," he said.

"What?"

"Oh, my God."

"What?" She had her dress on and was struggling with the zipper. She opened the door to see what had upset him.

He stood beside the bed naked, his boxers in his hand. "Why didn't you tell me?"

"Tell you what?"

"That you were a virgin, Lisa." He raked a hand through his black hair and it stood up in unruly waves. "I am so dense. I knew there was something I wasn't paying attention to. I'm sorry."

"For what?" Heart pounding, she turned back into the bathroom, found a comb in a drawer and tried unsuccessfully to tame her hair. Her inexperience shouldn't have to be embarrassing.

"For not knowing."

"What was to know? I didn't tell you because I didn't want it to be a big deal." Wherever she'd left her purse, she had a scrunchie. She moved through his room, ignoring him as he tried to step into his pants and follow her at the same time.

"It *is* a big deal." He grabbed his socks and shirt. "You'd never had sex before. I was your first partner and I didn't know."

She was ahead of him on the iron staircase. "I really didn't want you to know. And now I don't want to talk about it."

"Lisa."

"Please?" she said, finally pausing in the living room but not looking at him. "Please, Riley, can you just let it go?"

Behind her he was silent.

She picked up her handbag, found her hair tie and gathered her hair into a knot on her head. "Will you take me home now?"

"Of course. Whatever you want."

It was much more awkward putting their clothing and shoes back on than it had been taking them off. They descended the stairs and Riley opened the garage doors.

After he'd locked the place up, they were on their way back toward town. The ride was dark and silent, punctuated only by the burning looks she sensed him sending her way. She would never let him know how she really felt.

The streets of Thunder Canyon were deserted this time of night, and Riley drove directly to her house and parked in the drive.

One news van was parked across the street.

"Don't get out," she said. "I don't want the papers to have a picture of our good-night."

"Okay."

"Thanks for dinner. And the wine. And making those arrangements with the reporters."

He reached for her hand. "Lisa."

She looked at him finally. He was as handsome as ever. Mr. Cool. "We met before."

"Before what?"

"Before I inherited the Queen of Hearts."

His eyebrows rose in confusion. "We did?"

"Yes." Her heart chugged nervously, but she forced the words out anyway. "I was your chemistry tutor in high school."

For a moment she thought he was going to deny it, but then he nodded. "I remember having a tutor to get through that class. That was *you?*"

"It was me."

"Well. Funny how life comes around in a circle sometimes."

She didn't think there was anything funny about it. "Yeah."

"I'll call you."

"You'll see me at the mine tomorrow."

He released her hand and reached for her shoulder, but she opened the car door, turning on the overhead light. "Night."

Lisa hurried to her door, fumbled for her keys and let herself inside. Why she'd told him, she didn't know. She hadn't meant to ever let on.

Joey and Piper were excited to see her, sniffing her skirt and her feet to see where she'd been. She let them out back and peered around the corner of the house to see Riley's red car drive away.

Her first day and night as the new and improved Lisa had gone quite well, she thought, unwilling to acknowledge the awkwardness at the end. No one could possibly think this evening had been boring. It had been box-office, Julia Roberts exciting. Dogs petted and fed, she trudged upstairs, stripped out of the dress and got in the shower.

After she'd dried her hair and fought for a spot between her two pets in her bed, she relaxed against the pillows and sighed. At least now she did feel different. Still like a fake, but at least a more knowledgeable and experienced fake.

She smiled to herself. Experienced with none other than wealthy Thunder Canyon scion, Riley Douglas.

* * *

Lisa stared at the newspaper on Bernadine's desk the following morning. *The Shady Lady or the Lucky Lady?* the caption under two photographs read. The photograph on the left was a picture of Lily Divine that Lisa had never seen before. The dark-haired woman was garbed in the red dress now on display at the museum. Someone had retouched a black-and-white photograph to add color. Lily was smiling her confident smile and had been cropped out so that only the shoulder of the man beside her could be seen.

The picture on the right was present-day living color. Last-night color to be exact. It was Lisa in her red dress, smiling a self-pleased smile at the camera. A quick glance at the surroundings showed it to have been taken outside the restaurant.

One can see the resemblance between these two auburn-haired beauties, both residents of Thunder Canyon, both well-to-do women, both knockouts in red. Is there more than a physical resemblance between the two?

"What is that supposed to be implying?"

"Who knows?" Bernadine replied.

Lisa held the paper up for a better view. "Do I really look like her?"

"Well…yes."

Lisa smiled. "Not a bad thing."

"Not at all."

"What business do we have today?"

"We have a letter from a Logan Banks's attorney claiming that Logan is your cousin and entitled to his share of the Queen of Hearts."

"Never heard of him."

"Didn't think so, but we're checking him out anyway. We have to send a legal response."

Lisa poured herself a cup of coffee. "Isn't this about the fourth new cousin I've had?"

"Fifth. Great suit."

"Thanks. I did a little shopping. Oh, yeah…" She fished in her bag and pulled out the signed contracts. "He signed 'em."

Bernadine smoothed the papers on her desktop. "All the incorporation papers have gone through. We have our ID numbers and we're ready for business. Have you decided about Riley's loan offer?"

"Won't any bank in Thunder Canyon give me a loan now?"

"Bank loans require collateral. They'd ask for a share of the mine."

"Okay."

"The personal loan ties up less of your assets."

"But I don't want it to be personal."

"You don't want to owe Douglas."

"Exactly."

"Whatever you prefer. Want to have lunch?"

Lisa assured her she did, but added, "We'll have to be back for the state inspection at the mine this afternoon."

"What is it? Water quality?"

"It's basically a run-through of regulations since we're not pumping yet. They're going to check for proper storage of explosives, escape routes, ladders, marked ore shutes."

Bernadine turned to take papers from the printer on

the stand behind her. "Wow, you're really getting the hang of this."

"Riley's the one who's been learning it all and filling me in."

"A good right-hand man, eh?"

Right hand. Left hand. Good with both hands. Lisa simply nodded.

Bernadine took her to the Hitching Post for lunch. The place was filled with customers this time, and nearly all of them recognized Lisa. She was greeted with stares, wide-eyed interest and even a few friendly hellos.

Today's front page of the *Nugget* had already been framed and hung over the bar, near the painting of Lily.

"Well, if it isn't the Lucky Lady herself!" the bartender called from behind the polished cherrywood bar.

Several people clapped and cheered as Lisa and Bernadine made their way to a booth. Lisa smiled and gestured with what turned out like a parade wave—at least to her. Feeling silly, she dropped her hand.

Her cheeks felt flushed. "This is the first time I've actually let people see me," she said, in awe of their reactions. "I've been so caught up in hiding and running from the cameras, avoiding people in general, that I guess I just didn't know what their reactions would really be."

"You're the town celebrity."

"For now."

They ordered and ate. Occasionally someone stopped by their table to talk to Lisa or congratulate her. When Bernadine asked for their check, the waitress told her their lunch was on the house.

They headed for the mine in the lawyer's car, while Lisa grappled with her newly discovered status in town.

Lisa showed her ID to the security guards along the route, and when they arrived at the mine site, several cars were already parked there. Lisa recognized the Douglases' silver Town Car.

Riley was standing with a group of men, some in casual business dress, others in jeans and work shirts. He saw Lisa and Bernadine approach and turned to greet them. Her body tingled with intimate remembrance when he shook her hand.

He made introductions, and Lisa had to fight the urge to look up at him and gauge his expression. She'd dressed the part of a professional, in her navy pinstripe suit and white blouse. The men were treating her with respect, and she wasn't about to make a fool of herself by looking at Riley and revealing the emotions threatening to resurface.

He gave her curious sidelong looks she caught from the corner of her eye, but he kept up the professional front.

"What are they doing now?" she asked, shading her eyes against the sun. A group of men had moved away.

"Checking the pumps that will suck water from the mine's lower levels as we look for another vein."

"When will the actual mining begin?" Bernadine asked.

"As long as everything passes today's inspection, the mining will start first thing tomorrow."

A thrill of anticipation passed through Lisa. "It's really going to happen."

Riley nodded. "It is." He glanced at her. "You remember we have a meeting day after tomorrow?"

"It's on my calendar."

"You need to have a plan for how you're going to proceed with profits."

So much to think about and plan for, she thought. "Who knew a lot of money would be so much work to handle?"

"I'm going to strongly urge you to roll back initial profits into mine improvements and then acquire other mine properties in the vicinity."

"I'm sure you know best." There was no way Bernadine could know by their conversation or careful expressions that they'd been more than business partners last night. Nine hours ago they'd been naked and wrapped around each other like the strands of a licorice twist. The sun seemed warmer all of a sudden, and Lisa fanned herself with the checklist he'd handed her.

The men returned with their reports, and all were favorable. Riley thanked them and the different groups walked toward the cars.

"Lisa."

She stopped at Riley's call and motioned for Bernadine to walk on to the car ahead of her.

"I just wanted to ask how you were doing."

"I'm doing fine."

He glanced around. "We need to talk."

She refused to meet his eyes. She knew exactly what he wanted to talk about and she didn't feel the same compunction. "Poor timing, Riley."

"Not here. Will you meet me tonight?"

"I can't."

"Tomorrow, then?"

"I'll call you."

"Okay."

She walked to where Bernadine waited in the driver's seat of her car.

"What did you say to him?" the lawyer asked.

"Nothing."

"He looks like you told him his dog died."

"He doesn't have a dog."

"Hmm. Deduct points for that, huh?"

Lisa glanced from Bernadine to Riley as he strode toward his chauffeured car. Her stomach dipped a little at the sight of the man…at her intimate personal knowledge of the man…and at the indelible memory of what they'd shared.

She'd known going into that experience that it wasn't leading to a relationship. She'd been fine with that, as long as she had the experience…and the memory.

How did other women handle casual affairs? How would Lily have handled a lover? What should the new and improved Lisa do?

Lisa corrected her thinking. Riley was not her lover. He was a man to whom she'd been attracted. A man who'd never paid her the time of day until she'd inherited a fortune. And a man with whom she'd slept because she'd wanted to and because she could.

She could do anything she wanted. She could sleep with him again. She could choose not to.

She didn't *have* to do anything. Except be true to herself.

But there was something she could *not* do. And it was imperative she remember she was not Julia Roberts. She could *not* fall in love with Riley Douglas.

Chapter Eight

Emelda Ross's home was located on the western out-skirts of town. The only places farther out than hers were the ice rink and the Douglas ranch. Lisa still had unan-swered questions in her mind, and the only person she knew of who was left to ask was the elderly lady who told stories to children in the library.

A dog barked from inside the house as Lisa parked and approached. The elderly woman peered out the door, then stepped onto the porch. A small Jack Russell terrier darted from behind the skirt of her long floral dress and yipped as Lisa got closer.

"Hi, fella." Lisa knelt and held out her hand.

The dog loped down the stairs and stood sniffing the air warily. It then trotted over to Lisa and licked her wrist and her fingers.

She scratched the animal's ears. "What's his name?"

"Dog. What's yours?"

"Lisa Martin."

"Lisa Jane! Well, why didn't you say so? Look at you! Come on in. I have applesauce cake."

She stood and climbed the stairs. Dog's nails clicked on the porch stairs as the pet followed her. "I tried to call, but only got a busy signal."

"I take the nuisance off the hook when I nap." Miss Emelda led the way into her house and ushered Lisa into a huge kitchen that was as outdated as her own. She cut slices of cake and poured Lisa a glass of milk as though she was still ten years old. "What are you reading now, Lisa Jane? You were never big on the classics, as I recall."

Lisa smiled as she said, "I like romance novels and cozy mysteries."

Miss Emelda chuckled. "I've read a few of those myself." She seated herself on a nearby chair. "I see your picture in the paper every day." She winked. "I especially liked the red dress."

"Thanks."

"What brings you clear out here?"

Lisa tasted the cake, paused in reverence and let her taste buds recover before she replied. "I've been digging into my great-great-grandmother's past."

"Aha. Lily."

"I visited with Tildy Matheson, and she had journals that belonged to Catherine Douglas. I read those, and what I'm reading and hearing are entirely different slants to what is commonly told about Lily."

"I've heard the old stories myself," Miss Emelda said

with a sage nod. "I had an aunt who was friends with the Hardings' daughter."

"Lily and her husband's daughter you mean?"

"Yes. Everyone still refers to her as Lily Divine, but she lived out her life married to a Harding. Their daughter would have been your great-grandmother."

"That's exciting. Did your aunt ever speak of the Harding family?"

"Oh, my, yes. Lily Harding was a headstrong woman, ahead of her time and subject for much discussion over the years. Seems she had a sorry lot in life before she came to Thunder Canyon. Not sure about the whole of it, but the story goes that she didn't think a woman's plight should be birthing a baby every year or being cook and laundress to a husband and his hired men. Lily saw too much abuse and too many women treated as property, and it was her mission to help women in need of a new start."

"Had Lily been mistreated herself?"

"That I don't know. All the stories I learned about her are from after she settled here. Lily's daughter said Lily inherited a bordello from a dear friend and turned it into a saloon and boardinghouse. When Thunder Canyon sprang up as a small mining town, she used a golden opportunity to make herself a modest fortune by selling liquor to the miners."

This story made more sense to Lisa. She listened with fascination.

"Now, Nathaniel Harding was a bounty hunter, a man tired of roaming, and he hired on to clean up the town and the saloons. Nate and Lily butted heads a good many times before they fell in love and got married. My guess is they butted heads a few times afterward, as well," she said with a wink.

"What a romantic story."

Miss Emelda chuckled. "Your favorite kind."

"Was Lily ever truly a prostitute?"

"I really don't know what her life was like before she took over the Shady Lady and met Nate Harding. And if'n it was true, she wouldn't have told her daughter now, do you think?"

"No. I guess not. But even if that was in her past— and I might never know for sure—she made a fresh start and did a lot of good in her life."

"She did at that."

"Thanks, Miss Emelda. You've been a big help." She stood.

The older woman bustled to remove their plates. "You know I like to tell stories about the old days. Maybe you'll be the one to pass this one on."

"I will."

"Take some cake home with you. I have too much and I don't get a lot of company. If I put it on this plate, you'll have to bring it back soon."

"I'll be glad to do that. And anytime you need someone to take care of Dog for you, you just call me." Lisa fished in her purse for a business card and placed it on Miss Emelda's counter. "That's what I do, you know."

"I don't go out much, but if I do, I'll call."

Lisa carried the plate of cake to her Blazer and waved to Miss Emelda and Dog. The old woman's stories had always delighted her in her childhood, and this one had been even more special than all the rest because it revealed truths Lisa longed to know.

Even if she never knew the complete truth about Lily, she was never going to be ashamed or embarrassed to be related to her again. The woman had been smart enough to run her own business, compassionate enough to help other women, bold enough to think women should vote and confident enough to wear a red dress.

Lisa smiled to herself as she drove toward home.

Among a dozen messages on her machine was one from Riley: *"Lisa. Can we get together? Call me."*

His voice affected her as it always did, making her stomach dip. Should they get together? That was the question, but she didn't have a good answer. Lisa wasn't about to take any chances with her heart where this guy was concerned. She had to keep her wits about her and stay one step ahead of his game. She wasn't hoping for a happy ending with Riley Douglas. Maybe the wise thing would be a friendly ending. The sooner, the better.

Riley tossed a signed stack of papers on Marge's desk just as his cell phone rang. He reached in his jeans pocket and dug it out. *Lisa.*

"Hey."

"Hi. You called?"

Marge glanced up at him. He stepped into his office and closed the door. "Can we get together? How about dinner?"

"We have a meeting tomorrow. We'll see each other then."

"I know. This isn't business."

"I don't know, Riley." He sensed the hesitation in her voice.

She was giving him the brush-off? His head was so mixed up, he couldn't wrap a coherent thought around the woman. She'd shown up in that red dress and he'd lost his mind. What was wrong with him? He didn't get *involved.* He didn't lose his cool and he never, *never* deflowered virgins.

In his defense, he hadn't known she was a virgin until he'd seen the telltale signs afterward. It still made him a little weak in the knees when he thought about it. She'd waited all these years to have sex and then she'd chosen him. The fact stunned him. She didn't want to talk about it. Hell, she didn't even want to have dinner with him.

He got a little defensive. "Are you giving me the big kiss-off here? If I did something, let me know what it was, will you?"

"You didn't do anything I didn't want you to do," she answered.

"Are you talking about sex?" he asked.

"What are you talking about?"

He thrust his fingers into his hair and gripped his scalp in frustration. "I'm talking about you avoiding me now. *Since* we had sex."

"I'm not avoiding you."

"What do you call it when you hedge a dinner invitation?"

"I'm sorry, Riley, did we make some sort of a commitment that I don't know about?"

Her words gut-punched him more effectively than if

she'd been standing in front of him and swung a fist. He was sounding like a clingy high school girl, and she'd just given him the we're-just-friends line. He was swimming in uncharted waters here and he was concerned his sense of direction was going to get him lost. This had never—ever—happened to him before. "Never mind. I'll see you tomorrow."

Riley snapped his phone shut and stared at his office wall for a full minute, collecting himself. Fine. So she wasn't enamored yet. He'd be damned if he was going to let that deter him. Her lack of enthusiasm wasn't part of the plan.

But he still had a plan. And he was nothing if not persistent in getting what he wanted.

She couldn't help herself. Lisa hung the beige suit back on the hanger and dressed in a pair of black hipster pants with a cute silver chain belt and a blouse that only buttoned up as far as her cleavage. She had these Lily boobs, she might as well show them to their advantage.

Now the shoes took some getting used to. After living in tennis shoes, these backless little heels took some practice. But she was getting the hang of them. She'd spent an hour on her toenails last night and finally decided on red. Red went with everything and, well, it just plain looked sexy.

The bank loan Riley had helped arrange for her had gone through, and after their meeting today she was going to buy a car. She didn't know the first thing about car buying. Should she ask for advice? She was too frugal not to want to avoid being taken advantage of.

She drove the Blazer to the Douglases' downtown office, where Riley had asked her to meet him, thinking as she did that she wouldn't be driving the familiar beast much longer. No more breakdown worries. No more dead batteries in winter or repair bills she couldn't afford. The enormity of her new situation still took some getting used to, and she had to remind herself all the time.

A checkbook-size folder held closed with a rubber band lay on the console. Inside were all the coupons she'd clipped and filed and saved. For days she'd been looking at it, considering throwing it out, but had been unable to. Fifty cents was still fifty cents. Lisa laughed at herself and imagined the looks she'd get if she presented a coupon at the Super Saver Mart now that everyone knew she was the millionaire heiress.

She parked in the small lot and concentrated on walking smoothly all the way inside and up to the receptionist's desk. She did pretty well, if not breaking an ankle was any indication.

"Lisa Martin?" The slender, dark-haired woman greeted her with a smile. "It's so nice to meet you. I'm Connie Gray. Mr. Douglas asked me to show you right into his office."

Connie opened a gleaming wood door and ushered her into a room similar to Riley's home office.

Riley stood from behind a glass-topped desk. His gaze swept over her from head to toe and he seemed to struggle to maintain a professional expression. "Good morning, Miss Martin."

This was only the second time she'd seen him since

the other night, and she was bound and determined not to show any reaction or weakness. "Good morning."

"There are drinks set up on the table over there," Connie told her. "And I put out rolls and sandwiches. Please help yourself." She smiled and closed the door behind her.

"Is it just us?" Lisa asked.

"Yes. You look great."

"Thanks." She made her way to the long table and placed two of the delicate sandwiches and a cinnamon roll on a gold-edged white china plate. "Ever heard of disposable plates?"

"Connie takes care of all that."

"Like Marge does at your other office."

"Yes."

"Do they know each other?"

"Yes, why?"

She seated herself at a table and tried a sandwich. "Mmm, awesome chicken-and-walnut mixture." Then answered him with, "Just wondering. What are we deciding today?"

He brought a couple of folders and an envelope from his desk and sat across from her. Within half an hour he'd explained financial details regarding the mine's initial operation and advised her on the best courses of action. "You do still trust me to advise you, don't you, Lisa?"

"Do I have reason not to?"

"I give you my word I'll consider each action as though this was my own money. I'll use the best of my ability to steer you toward decisions that will benefit your corporation. I intend to show you every penny of income and expense and to offer you my best advice on generating profits."

"Your word is good enough for me," she replied easily. It was in his best interest to make her money since he wanted to share in it. She'd been born at night, but it hadn't been last night.

A roll and a cup of coffee later, their business was concluded. He was good at this money-managing stuff.

His intercom beeped and Connie said, "Mine foreman is on line one, Mr. Douglas. He says it's important."

Riley got up and stood beside his desk to push the speakerphone button. "Douglas here."

"Mr. Douglas." The man's voice was clear. "I couldn't reach anyone at Miss Martin's number. The two of you might want to be here when we haul this car out into the sunlight."

Riley met Lisa's eyes. "We'll be there."

He clicked off the phone and pressed the intercom button. "Connie, have the driver bring the car around, please."

"What's going on?" Lisa asked.

"This is it. The first of the ore. It's been right there waiting for us to have everything in place. Let's go."

"Oh, wow! This is exciting." Lisa pointed to the table. "Let's grab a few of those sandwiches for the road. They'll tide us over."

He watched her pile several sandwiches on a plate and cover them with a cloth napkin.

"What?" she said. "I'll return your napkin."

"Take all the napkins if you want. I don't care."

"Then what are you looking at?"

"You."

Lisa looked away, momentarily flustered. "Let's go."

They headed out past the receptionist and onto the street, where the chauffeur waited beside the Town Car. "Where to, Mr. Douglas?"

"The mine."

They got in and got settled. She placed the plate of sandwiches on the seat between them, and he looked out the window with a grin.

"Great picture in the paper. The one of you in the red dress," he said.

She hadn't minded it. She gave him a sideways glance and grinned. "It was okay."

He looked back. "Did you know the AP picked it up?"

"Associated Press?"

"Uh-huh. Chad Falkner made himself a pretty penny selling it to *People*."

"No way!"

"I'd watch for the next issue."

"Stop it." He was putting her on, and she wasn't falling for it. The thought of plain-Jane Lisa Martin's photo beside Jennifer Aniston's was ludicrous.

"So, we're on our way to see gold, is that right?"

"That's what's excavated from a gold mine."

"It's going to be real now." She looked out the window at the passing scenery, excited now in spite of herself. "What do you have on your schedule this afternoon?"

He thought a minute. "Paperwork for the ski resort."

"Anything you can work around?"

"Yes, why?"

She looked at him. "I want to go buy a car. Maybe you could advise me. I don't want to pay more than I should."

"Do you know what you want?"

"Not really."

He tapped his fingers on his knee. "Were you thinking of going to Billings? Are you ordering or buying from a showroom?"

She shrugged. "I have no idea."

"I'll come with you. We'll stop by the ranch to get my car on the way back," Riley said. "I rode in with my dad this morning."

"What about the Blazer? Won't I need it for the trade-in?"

"Lisa." He cocked a brow. "Get serious."

"What?"

"You're not going to get a trade-in on that thing. Besides, it won't make it that far."

"What will I do with it, then?"

"Call a scrap-metal dealer? Have a bonfire?"

She gave him a sideways look. It was fine for her to belittle her own vehicle, but she didn't like the verbal degradation coming from him. "I'll have you know that Blazer got me where I needed to go for the last ten years…*most* of the time."

"So it has sentimental value?"

"Some."

He tilted his head. "I hear you can have a vehicle smashed down into a coffee table."

"Now there's an idea."

They shared a laugh just as the driver pulled up to the last security point.

When they reached the mine, the flurry of activity amazed Lisa. There were workmen and trucks and all manner of tools and apparatus she'd never seen before.

The foreman dashed out to meet them. "It's up. Wait till you see!"

He led them to a metal cart filled with chunks of ore taken from the mine's interior.

"There you go, Lisa," Riley said, urging her forward. "There's your gold."

She stared at hunks of rock with gleaming fissures and exposed nuggets. Sunlight caught the exposed veins and gold glittered.

Riley asked for a hammer and knocked off a piece. Turning to Lisa, he held it out, then dropped it into her extended palm.

The chunk of gold he'd given her was as big as a plum and heavy. She held it out so the light caught it, then glanced at each person in the gathering. Smiles creased every face.

Someone let out a whoop, and the rest joined in. Lisa found herself swept into Riley's arms and spun around in a circle. When he set her down, the men crowded around her with excited congratulations. The whole thing still seemed surreal.

"Now do you believe you're wealthy?" Riley asked sometime later as they walked back to the car. "You owned the gold all along, but now you've seen it."

"It's more real, that's for sure." She still held the nugget.

The driver took them to Riley's, where they got his car. She dropped the piece of gold into her purse and selected a CD. Riley showed her how to load the unfamiliar machine and press Start.

"I think I'll get a car with one of these players."

The sandwiches ran out long before they reached Billings, and Riley drove through a fast-food place on the highway to order a burger and a soda. Lisa got a shake.

When they reached the city, he pulled onto the first car lot he came to, which happened to be a BMW dealership.

A young salesman spotted the red Jaguar and nearly ran out to greet them. "Hi! Are you looking for anything in particular today?"

"I just want to look," Lisa told the salesman pointedly.

"Go right ahead." The young man handed Riley a business card. "I'm Jamie. I'll be glad to help you if you have any questions."

Lisa test-drove half a dozen cars, but felt her eyes bug out of her head when she asked how much the price was on the one she liked the best.

"It's a *car*," she said to Riley, but the salesman was within hearing distance, so she lowered her voice. "I could pay the national debt with that much money. Or build a children's hospital."

"A hospital." Riley raised a brow and studied her.

"Well, a clinic. Hey, an animal shelter. Why on earth would I want to spend that much money on a car?"

"It's not just a car, Lisa, it's a BMW. Like mine is a Jag. It's going to cost more money than a midsize family sedan or an economy car. People buy them because they can afford to. A car like this is about image. You're a wealthy woman now. The cars you choose reflect you and the way you want to be seen."

"Afford it or not—image or no—it's a waste of money. I want to go somewhere where I won't feel like I'm throwing money away."

"It's not throwing money away, it's an investment."

"No, a stock is an investment. A car is transportation."

"Why'd you bring me, then? To make me crazy?"

"No, I read somewhere that a man can negotiate for a better deal than a woman. Did you notice he gave his card to *you,* when I'm the one who said I wanted to look?"

He tilted his head to indicate he had.

"*And* I brought you because I don't know cars."

At that remark he stared at her pointedly.

"I don't know cars, but I know I don't want one this expensive."

"Okay." He turned to the salesman. "Thanks for your help. We're going to look around a little more."

The next dealership was more like it. It still seemed an extravagance to buy a brand-new car when slightly used or even mildly dented would get her around just as well, but she fell in love with a new Blazer, gold in color.

"You said image, and this is image. It's *gold,*" she said to Riley with a grin.

"But you've driven a Blazer for the last—how long?—twelve years? Don't you want something different—sportier maybe?"

"I need four-wheel drive in winter. It's practical."

"I agree, but you could get both. This plus something sporty."

She directed her palm at his suggestion. "Don't. Uh-uh. One is plenty. Baby steps, remember?"

The salesman was nearly jumping up and down over

the sale with a check in full as payment, but when Riley started talking about two vehicles, she thought the fellow was going to hyperventilate.

"Easy." Lisa turned to him and explained in a serious tone, "I'm only getting the Blazer. Period."

The man looked to Riley, who shrugged. "She's calling the shots."

It took longer than she thought it should have for the transaction and for the service department to do their thing. She was itching to get the keys and her bill of sale.

"How about dinner?" Riley asked. "By the time we get back, they'll have your new wheels ready."

She had asked him to take time from his day to help her make this choice, though she'd pretty much made all the decisions herself. Riley was her measuring stick, however, and as long as she stayed just under his suggestions, she felt comfortable. She owed him for his patience. "Okay."

"Let's go make sure they didn't sell my car while I was looking with you."

With a grin Lisa joined him. The salesman had been disappointed when he'd learned Riley's Jag was not a trade-in.

"Where to?" she asked a few minutes later.

"What are you hungry for?"

"I'll eat anything."

"I've noticed."

She cast a frown his direction. "You'd rather take a picky eater to dinner?"

"Definitely not. Unless it was you. I just want to take you to dinner."

"Good cover."

"Yeah."

Lisa chose the restaurant—a casual steak house with a salad bar—and paid for their meals while Riley was using the restroom.

"Why'd you do that?" he asked as they took seats and the waitress handed them plates.

"You helped me today. It was the least I could do."

The waitress walked away.

Lisa leaned forward. "Besides, I'm rich."

She got up and went to prepare her salad. Riley followed and stood beside her. "This is a date, so I'm supposed to pay."

She barely glanced up from her plate of lettuce. "Who says?"

"Who says what? That it's a date or that I'm supposed to pay?"

"Both."

He made his salad and returned to the table with her. "You don't make anything easy, do you?"

She hoped not. It was her goal to stay a giant leap ahead of him at all times. She was not going to be sucked into his scheme. She'd always been attracted to him, so she had that working against her. She could never let him know how she really felt about him. But besides that she was having the time of her life.

"Remember this Saturday evening is the groundbreaking reception," he said.

She had forgotten.

"You agreed to come."

She nodded. "I'll drive myself."

Their dinners arrived. "Have you scheduled your interview?"

"I've been putting it off. I was thinking I'd call to-morrow and arrange it. If they keep up their part of the deal and leave me alone for a week, it will be pure bliss."

"You can always use my cabin. Feel free to take your dogs and stay as long as you like. There's only one lock—the one that gets you in through the garage—and I'll have a key made for you."

The offer was so tempting, she hadn't allowed her-self to think about it. Time away from prying eyes would be welcome. Maybe she had a few qualms about return-ing to the place where she'd lost her virginity, but she'd have to deal with that eventually. "I don't know how I'd find it myself."

"I could take you out. Or lead the way." He looked up. "If you planned to take off during the week the reporters were leaving you alone, they wouldn't see you to follow."

She leaned forward. "The last day of the reprieve I could go out and take as many days undiscovered as I like."

He nodded.

Lisa laid down her fork. "How long can this last, Riley? I mean, wouldn't you think they'd be bored with this whole story by now?"

"There's something fascinating about the whole rags-to-riches story," he said, then paused with an apologetic look. "Not that you wore rags, but—"

"I get it."

"Your evasiveness is like an aphrodisiac to them," he said. Maybe he knew firsthand?

"I've heard of celebrities who go ahead and stop and pose for photos and then the paparazzi leave them alone because they got what they wanted."

He nodded as he finished his steak.

"Maybe this interview will have that effect."

"That's what we're counting on."

He had been a big help. She'd have been even more lost without him. But after what had transpired between them, things were more tense. Lisa had wanted what had happened. She was honest with herself—she could admit she wanted more. She just had to guard her heart. That was her first priority. If she could do that and still let him as physically close as she sensed him working toward, she would have it all.

"Saturday night," she said.

Riley had finished eating, and the waitress poured them cups of coffee. He smiled at the woman, and she blushed as she walked away.

"Saturday night," he prompted.

"Could you devise a way to come back to my place after the reception? You never did get to look at those journals."

He thought a minute. "You'll be driving yourself to the ranch, so they'll be following you home. What if I leave ahead of you and get to your place first? I can park a block or so away."

She dug in her purse, smiled when her fingers touched the gold nugget and came up with her extra key. "The dogs won't know you, so I'll leave them in their runs out back. You'll have to let yourself in the front."

She met his eyes and warmth diffused her face, neck

and chest. They were methodically planning a night together and they both knew it. Images of their last time
snagged Lisa's breath and made her heart jump errati-
cally. She was in control and she was not a coward. So
much of her life had already slipped by that she wasn't
willing to miss any more. She would only regret her actions if she let her heart get involved or if she didn't grab
on to this opportunity.

   Lisa didn't want any regrets.

Chapter Nine

It's All About Gold for the Lady In Red.

Bernadine had spotted Lisa walking an Irish setter in the park, slid out of her car and run all the way, waving a magazine.

Lisa gave the woman a wide-eyed once-over, taking in her heels and taupe linen suit. "What's this all about?"

"My partner brought this to me. Look!" She showed Lisa the front cover of *People* magazine with its usual assortment of stars and captions. In the lower left-hand corner beside Paris Hilton in a slinky pink gown was a picture of Lisa in her red dress. Lisa looked twice, then grabbed the magazine from Bernadine's hand to get a closer look.

"It's me." She looked up, then back at the glossy cover. "Oh, my—it's *me!*"

"The story's on page nineteen," her lawyer said breathlessly.

Lisa flipped the pages until she came to the article that took an entire page. Half was a montage of color photos, the other half caption and text. "It's all about gold for the lady in red," she read aloud, her voice trembling. She went on to read the story, which played on local girl striking the mother lode. Lily Divine was of course mentioned, and there were quotes made by neighbors and people Lisa barely knew.

Mrs. Carlson was quoted as saying, "She's always been a shy girl. Keeps to herself and dotes on those dogs of hers." There was a small picture of her with Joey and Piper, taken from a distance, and it looked as though she was in her own yard. The biggest pictures were of her in the red dress—one with Riley at her side as they strode toward the cameramen outside the restaurant in Billings.

"Riley told me Chad Falkner sold pictures to *People,* but I thought he was putting me on." She closed the magazine and stared at her photo next to Paris Hilton's. "I don't *believe* this."

"You're a phenomenon, kiddo. Everyone aspires to win the lottery or the sweepstakes and become an overnight millionaire. You're an American dream come true."

"This is awful," Lisa said as the reality of this latest publicity hit her full force.

"What? You put Thunder Canyon in the spotlight."

"What does this mean, though? Will even more reporters come looking for me now?" She glanced around in dread.

Bernadine shrugged. "I don't know."

"Come on, Brinkley," Lisa said to the setter. "Let's get you home. I have phone calls to make." She headed for her new Blazer, and Bernadine kept pace beside her. "I'm going to schedule that interview Riley arranged. Will you be there?"

"Sure."

"Okay, good. And then I'm going to disappear for a while."

"You'll have to stay in touch with me. Where will you go?"

"I have a place in mind."

Bernadine handed her the magazine and admired the new SUV. "Nice vehicle."

"Thanks."

After taking the setter back, she went home and called Chad Falkner and the other local reporters to schedule an interview for the next day. She wanted the taping to take place in her home, where she was comfortable and where they could appease their fascination once and for all.

The salesgirl in Billings had given her a business card, so she called her and told her she needed something to wear on Saturday. The young woman had ordered a few things especially for her and offered to keep the store open for Lisa to try them on that evening. "Or I can come to Thunder Canyon," she told her. "No problem."

"No, I'll be there," Lisa told her. "I have a new car to drive now."

Gwen had specially ordered at least thirty dresses and as many casual outfits for Lisa to try on and showed Lisa as soon as she arrived. She had excellent taste, had picked up on Lisa's new metamorphosis and personality and had chosen garments accordingly.

"I saw you in the dress in the papers—and on the cover of *People*," she told her excitedly. "I told you that was a great choice."

"You did. I need something equally as…"

"Sexy?"

Lisa blushed. "Spectacular, anyway, for Saturday."

"Look at this." Gwen took the tissue from a slinky gown in shades of aqua and teal with tinges that shimmered pink in the light. "It reminds me of a butterfly," she told Lisa. "And so do you."

Lisa slipped into the dress and turned in front of the mirror. The garment dipped revealingly low in the back, and the side was slit up her thigh. Staring at herself, Lisa felt light and elusive—exactly the impression she wanted to convey. "You're a genius," she told Gwen. "I could never have shopped for myself this well."

"I also took the liberty of finding accessories," Gwen said hesitantly. "If I've overstepped bounds here, just say so. I can send back anything you don't want."

"Not at all. I need your help. I've never done this before."

"Lisa, you're beautiful. You look great in gorgeous clothes and you can afford the best. Allow yourself to enjoy this."

"I think I am. Thanks."

Gwen showed her the handbag and shoes she'd chosen, as well as sparkling butterfly pins for her hair. "What do you think?"

"That you've spoiled me and I'll need to hire you."

Gwen laughed. "That would be a dream job. I should be so lucky."

Lisa looked in the mirror again. "Think Paris Hilton has a personal shopper?"

"From what I've seen, she likes doing all her own shopping. She has a much different background and has always been a spoiled rich girl. Besides, designers are chasing after her to wear their stuff."

"I'm really getting into this," Lisa confessed.

"And why not? I heard about the big event Saturday night. I assume you're attending the ski-resort ground-breaking reception."

"Yes. I've never been around people like the Douglases and the mayor before. If I look good, I'll feel confident."

"You look good, honey. You definitely look good."

Dressed in her new clothing and driving her new Blazer, Lisa arrived at the Lazy D on Saturday night feeling more like Cinderella than ever before. She'd taken every measure she could to assure she'd look the part of the town's rich girl, but apprehension still fluttered in her chest. She pulled up to the house, and a parking attendant assisted her out, then took the keys to move her vehicle.

Lisa had been to the Douglas house before but never at night, when the windows were lit from within and strings of lights draped from posts to lead the way to the entrance. The door opened as she reached it, and a man in a tux motioned for her to enter.

"Good evening, miss."

She stood in the two-story foyer and glanced at the grand sweeping staircase, then at the room to her left.

Voices and the sound of stringed music carried out to the foyer.

Adele Douglas greeted her in the opening to the enormous room. "Good evening, Lisa," she said with a smile. "How nice to see you again. You're quite the news about town. I don't know when there's been so much excitement. You look so lovely, dear, I can hardly take it all in."

"Hello, Mrs. Douglas."

"Adele, *please*. Mrs. Douglas was my mother-in-law."

Adele had always reminded Lisa of a gracefully aging Meryl Streep in her serenity and quiet dignity. She was one person who wasn't treating Lisa any differently than she ever had. She'd always been warm and gracious.

Lisa recalled Riley's revelation about his father's affair and how Adele had only recently learned of her husband's illegitimate adult son. Only a classy woman such as this could forgive and accept and move on. "I never thought I'd be here for an occasion like this," Lisa admitted. "I'll have to have a moment with Derek before the evening's over."

Adele laughed. "You'll find him in the family room at the back of the house. It's his hiding place when we have company. I know he'll enjoy your attention, though."

"I'll look for him."

Caleb approached Lisa. He extended a hand and closed it over hers in a firm hold. "Riley told me you'd be coming. This is an exciting evening for us. We're finally going to see the resort take shape."

"I know Riley's excited about the project," she replied. "It's going to be a boost to our town's economy."

"That and the gold mine," he said with a wink. "You hold an important position now, as well, supplying jobs and channeling money into the community. Riley is the best man to help you with that. He's handled our finances for years now and he has a nose for making money."

"And spending it," she said under her breath.

She sensed someone at her side and turned to find Riley in a white shirt and black suit. His appreciative gaze told her the dress was another hit.

"There's nothing my boy doesn't know about finance," Caleb went on. "Trust him, and he'll steer you right. He's a good dancer, too."

The string quartet, which was set up in the corner, had begun a new piece, and Caleb gestured for Riley to escort her to the area set aside for dancing. Riley took her hand and led her to where Emily Stanton and Brad Vaughn danced. Emily introduced Lisa to her new husband.

Lisa hadn't danced since gym class in high school, but Riley put her at ease and smoothly led her in the steps. With one hand on her bare back and the other holding her hand, electricity sparked between them. He was more handsome than ever in his formal suit and tie. Looking at him made it difficult to breathe.

She was bold and confident when she'd made her plans, but when he held her like this, her self-assurance wavered. It took all of her considerable will to erect adequate barriers of protection. Riley was the demolition man, and she had to keep reconstructing the fortress that guarded her feelings.

"You do trust me, don't you, Lisa?" His voice was low and seductive.

"Of course I do." She trusted him to be persistent and persuasive. She trusted him to behave like the man he was born and bred to be. She trusted him to keep her on her toes.

"You're doing a number on me in that dress, you know."

"That's what I like to hear."

He glanced down, his gaze traveling to her cleavage. "I can't help wondering what you have on underneath."

Her nipples tightened, and warmth tingled in surprising places. "Shall I tell you?"

He was silent a moment. "I'll just keep wondering."

She smiled and glanced away. "Suit yourself."

For the first time she noticed that the two of them were cause for attention. Several curious looks were being cast their way. Adele and another woman were studying them with interest as they danced, and Lisa thought she spotted jealousy on a few female faces.

Her emotions ranged from pride to unease. "People are watching us."

"They're watching you. You're beautiful."

He'd told her that before. She glanced up, hoping to see the truth in his expression. He found her beautiful now, and yes, she had changed her appearance, but she was the same girl she'd been in high school—or even a month ago. He hadn't given her a second glance then. How much of the attraction was her transformation and how much was money?

"I did the interview Thursday," she told him.

"How'd it go?"

"Good. Bernadine came. I haven't been followed since. I wasn't even followed here tonight."

"So you think you have until next Thursday free and clear?"

She nodded. "Seems they're keeping their word."

"You can make arrangements with your customers and spend some time at the cabin, then."

"I think I will."

Riley changed the topic, filling her in on the identities of several of the partygoers. They ended the dance and he introduced her to his acquaintances. But underneath it all simmered the rising tension of what they'd planned for afterward. The night ahead never left Lisa's mind and she doubted from the looks he gave her that it left Riley's, either.

"Miss Lisa Jane," a man said jovially from beside her.

Lisa turned to discover portly Mayor Brookhurst. She'd met him face-to-face the day she'd claimed the deed.

"Hello, Mayor."

"You're the belle of the ball tonight," he told her. "May I have a dance?"

She glanced uncomfortably at Riley but said, "Certainly."

The mayor wasn't nearly as smooth a dancer as Riley. She didn't like suspecting that part of his reason in asking her had been to get close, but her dress was little more than tissue paper between her skin and the mayor's suit. It had been sensual with Riley as her dance partner. With the mayor it felt obscene.

After the song ended she excused herself as quickly as possible and sought out Bernadine, who was visiting with another woman.

"Lisa, this is Olivia Chester," the lawyer said. "She's our local ob-gyn."

Lisa greeted the pretty Native American woman she guessed to be in her forties.

"I've followed all the excitement about the gold mine," Olivia told her. Then she grinned and said, "Kind of hard not to."

Caleb approached Lisa then. "I have someone I want you to meet."

She excused herself and joined him. He led her to a small group. A young man and woman turned at his approach.

"Lisa, this is my son and his new wife, Justin and my adopted daughter, Katie."

"Lisa and I have met, of course," Katie told Caleb and greeted Lisa warmly. "Lisa has come into the library often."

"Nice to meet you, Lisa." Justin was tall and broad shouldered like Riley, his hair the same gleaming obsidian and his eyes held a similar intensity. The resemblance between the two half brothers was amazing. "I would have been able to recognize you without the introduction," she said.

"Both my sons are handsome devils, aren't they?" Caleb said proudly.

"That they are," Katie agreed, wrapping her arm around Justin's waist and smiling up at him.

Lisa imagined that Caleb had once been as tall and

virile-looking as his sons, too, because he was still a handsome man.

"Where is Riley, anyway?" Katie asked. "I never see much of him anymore." She spotted him, caught his eye and gestured for Riley to join them.

Lisa sensed Riley's unease as soon as he approached and stood with the group. She'd heard the pain in his voice when he'd spoken of this newly discovered brother. It had been plain that he still had a ways to go in accepting the situation.

Caleb behaved as though things couldn't have been more normal, however. "What a treat to have you all together. Adele and I are planning a family shindig soon. You're invited, Lisa. We'd love to have you join us."

"Well, thank you," she said uncomfortably. "I'll have to see if I can make it."

"Of course you can make it. You'll be there."

Lisa exchanged a look with Katie, who simply smiled as though she was used to the older man's overbearing manner.

"Excuse us now," Riley said. "I want to introduce Lisa to Phil."

Lisa met his friend and financial advisor, Phil Wagner, and while the two men stood talking, she slipped away and headed toward the back of the house.

Meeting all those strangers and trying to remember names and keep smiling was exhausting. The "family room," as Adele had called it, was an immense room with Oriental rugs, a pool table, fireplace, sofa and love seats.

At Lisa's entry, Derek—Adele's enormous white

poodle—roused from his resting place on the floor, sniffed the air hesitantly, then came forward to greet her with a lick.

"Hey, boy. How are you doing?" The white poodle wore a red bandanna around his neck and, as Riley had so adeptly described, his fur was cut into ridiculous pom-poms. Quite undignified for such a mannerly and handsome animal but not his fault, as she still maintained. Derek's fur was so thick, she had to bury her fingers in it to scratch him.

"Smart of you to find a quiet place to hide out. Wouldn't mind joining you, actually. You're smelling my dogs, aren't you? Wonder what they'd make of you."

She eased down onto the sofa and slipped off her shoes. Derek sat at her knees and seemed to enjoy her company and a lengthy head scratch by closing his eyes.

Sometime later the dog eased onto the sofa beside her, and they were enjoying the quiet time together when Riley found her. "There you are. Mother said I'd find you here."

"Derek and I are hanging out."

Riley glanced at the dog that barely seemed to notice his arrival. "What do you see in him, anyway?"

"He's affectionate. And intelligent. He's back here away from the crazies, isn't he? Don't give me your respect theory again. Respect is a two-way street. I doubt he thinks much of you either."

Derek opened eyes to slits to look at Riley at that moment, as though assessing the man.

Riley perched on Lisa's other side.

"So, Derek, what do you think of Riley?" she asked. "Would you trust him with your best rawhide strip? He could turn it into a steak for you. He has a way with investing." The dog tilted his head in keen interest as she spoke.

Riley chuckled and leaned forward to kiss her. She lifted her face to meet him. A sigh escaped her.

"You're a nut, you know that?" he said, gazing at her fondly.

"Be that as it may, I think you should give Derek a chance before it's too late for the two of you."

"How's it going to be too late?"

"Don't want him to hear this, but ogdays on'tday ivelay ongerlay anthay ifteenfay or osay earsyay."

"What did you just say?"

"You don't understand pig latin?"

"Sorry, I had a French tutor."

She leaned forward and whispered in his ear. "Dogs don't live longer than fifteen or so years. Your bonding is going to have to happen now."

She sat back and he studied her eyes with amusement flickering in his. "There's no one else I would do this for, you know that, don't you?"

She shrugged mischievously.

He turned and faced the dog. "So, Derek. May I call you Derek? It's come to my attention that I haven't given you a fair chance. I'd like to correct that. Can we be friends?"

The dog merely looked at him. Lisa had stopped scratching his head, and the animal looked expectantly from Lisa back to Riley.

Riley extended a hand.

Derek licked it.

Riley rubbed Derek's head.

"There, isn't that better?" Lisa raised up and kissed Riley's cheek.

He turned his face and reached his left arm around her back to bring her closer. Their lips met in a warm, melding crush of eager anticipation. His kiss had the same narcotic effect as the first time. She could easily become a Riley junkie.

A kiss wasn't enough. Two kisses weren't enough. She pressed her palm against the crisp starched front of his shirt and felt his warm flesh and hard muscle beneath. More. She wanted more.

She felt something warm and damp but completely out of place and realized Derek was licking her bare toes. "I think it's time to go."

Riley helped her to her feet and paused to address the dog. "Excuse us now. I'm not sharing her for the rest of the night."

She smiled and gave the dog a last affectionate pat.

Riley took her hand and they fled out the back door.

As they'd planned, Riley used one of his father's plain sedans and left first. Lisa waited fifteen tense minutes before following.

Surprisingly no one followed her. The reporters had been good for their word. Her heart pounded in a silly girlish flutter every time she imagined Riley at her house. Riley in her bed. But she calmed her giddiness and forced herself to think rationally. This was a temporary diversion. She was allowing him to think he was pulling one over on her. But no matter what, she would not let him know her feelings and she would not let her feelings get out of control.

She parked in her driveway and got out of her Blazer. At the back fence, the dogs whined. She walked toward the back, unlocked the gate and entered the yard.

She let the boys free from their run, and they ran in circles around her, pausing to sniff her feet and skirt and hands, keenly aware of the other dog scent.

"Be on your best behavior, boys. We have a guest."

She unlocked the back door and pushed it open. The light she'd left on over the sink partially illuminated the room.

"Riley?" she called.

"In here."

A light came on in the living room.

"I waited to turn on a lamp." His footsteps sounded in the hallway.

The dogs turned in that direction, and Piper let out an ear-piercing bark followed by a volley of others.

"Piper. Hush," she told him. "It's okay." Lisa hurried to meet Riley in the kitchen entryway, where she stood in front of him and turned to the dogs. Riley held a bottle of wine.

"Joey, Piper, you remember Riley. You met him once before." She took Riley's arm and leaned into him to show her pets the man was a friend.

Tail wagging, Joey came forward and sniffed Riley's trouser legs, then his crotch.

Riley took a wary step back.

"Sorry," Lisa said without embarrassment. One couldn't spend much time around dogs without becoming immune to their natures.

Riley extended a hand and Joey sniffed it, then allowed the man to pet his head and scratch behind his ears.

Piper, on the other hand, remained several feet away and growled low in his throat.

Lisa spent another five minutes coaxing the dark golden retriever to relax his guard and accept Riley, but the dog remained agitated.

Finally she ordered the animal to lie down on the kitchen rug and she got two glasses from the cupboard.

"Sorry they're not fancy," she said, indicating the tall, thin glasses with faded irises on the sides. She glanced at the bottle. "I don't have a corkscrew."

"I calculated for that." Reaching into the pocket of his suit coat, he pulled one out. "Brought one from the house."

"That's probably Piper's problem. He sensed you were carrying a weapon."

He cocked a brow to give her a skeptical look, then opened the wine and poured the glasses half-full. "What shall we drink to?"

Lisa blinked and studied him in the dim light. "I don't know."

He held up his glass and she did the same. "To second chances."

What he meant by that, she wasn't sure. He might have meant any number of things. His father and his half brother came to mind. He could be teasing her about Derek. Or he might be talking sex and toasting their second time together. Her stomach dipped at that possibility.

In the next second, the burning look in his blue eyes made her think that's exactly what he was talking about.

She sipped the wine.

He watched and did the same.

Riley took her glass and set both on the red Formica table. Without another word he pulled her into his arms and kissed her senseless.

Lisa met every brush of his lips and thrust of his tongue eagerly. She wrapped one arm around his neck and pulled herself closer.

Riley used his fingertips on the bare skin of her back to create shivers and raise her level of excitement. "You're not wearing a bra."

"You wanted me to let you wonder."

"I've figured it out. You couldn't be wearing one with this dress."

She'd let Gwen talk her into the thong this time, too. Lisa still had a surprise or two left.

"Why are you smiling?"

"You'll see."

"When?"

She reached up and loosened the knot in his tie until she could edge it away from his collar and off over his head. "Soon."

He took off his suit coat and she unbuttoned his shirt.

He wore the familiar white T-shirt, and she tugged it from the waistband of his trousers. He crossed his arms and yanked it off over his head.

Lisa pressed languid kisses against his chest.

"Where's your room?"

"Upstairs."

He picked up their glasses. "Lead the way."

Chapter Ten

She left the light on over the sink as well as the lamp he'd turned on in the living room and led the way up the shadowed staircase. She'd climbed these stairs hundreds of times, maybe thousands. Never with a man.

Well, no man except Wendell Carlton, the aged handyman her grandmother had occasionally hired to fix things. Wendell didn't count. Riley wasn't here to fix a leak or caulk a tub. Her knees got weak at the thought of him in her room.

After entering her bedroom, she turned on the painted-glass lamp on her dresser, knowing it would just barely illuminate.

Riley glanced at the antique furniture, the old-fashioned metal bed frame with its chenille spread and folded quilt. Her pillowcases were delicately embroidered and edged with crocheted lace. She knew how different her home was from his, how much their tastes contrasted. This was who she was, and him knowing it made her uncomfortably vulnerable.

He set the glasses on her painted night table and eyed her vintage bed. "Is that frame sturdy?"

"I guess we'll find out."

He grinned.

She turned so he could unzip her dress. He lowered the zipper and she stepped out of the garment, draping it over the cedar chest. She took a fortifying breath and turned back to see his reaction.

Riley was looking at her as if he couldn't drag his gaze away. Finally he spoke. "Wow."

She picked up her glass and let her gaze seduce him. "You're overdressed."

He sat on her bed to remove his shoes and socks, then stood and stepped out of his trousers. Still wearing a pair of snug-fitting gray boxer-briefs, he took his own glass and downed the liquid in one swallow. "Want more? I can go get the bottle."

She shook her head no, sipped her wine slowly, then set her glass aside and eased onto the bed. "Maybe later."

Riley kept a rein on his hunger. She knew exactly what she was doing. This woman strove to drive him crazy. She was a seductress in every way. If she'd told him she was a virgin, he probably wouldn't have believed her. But he'd learned firsthand. The thought still tied him in knots. And she wouldn't talk about it.

Something primitively male and possessive and old-fashioned puffed up inside him at the prideful knowledge that he was the only man who'd ever made love to her.

Just looking at Lisa now made his chest swell, and feelings he'd never known overcame him. The emotions weren't anything he wanted to acknowledge. They weren't anything he knew or understood.

She eased the covers back and stretched out on the bed.

But they were sensations that had begun to control him.

She was an anomaly, a siren and an innocent in one fabulous package.

She consumed his thoughts.

"Like the thong?" she asked.

"Love it."

"Now that you've seen it, I really want to toss it."

He laughed. "Go right ahead."

He loved her.

She eased the scrap of satin down her hips and legs and gave it a fling.

He lost a slat in the rickety footbridge between his brain centers, and his thoughts swung by a precarious thread. *Not part of the plan,* his head told him.

Doesn't matter, his body responded.

You're in perilous territory here. That word shouldn't have been in your mental vocabulary.

Just a slip. I didn't mean it. And I certainly didn't say it.

"What are you waiting for?" she asked.

"Just appreciating the view."

She propped her head on one hand. "Well, share the experience, then."

Riley stripped off his briefs and climbed onto the bed, not caring how small the mattress was or that the metal headboard creaked with his weight. All he wanted was to be close to Lisa.

A low growl thwarted his next move, however, and he raised his head to find the dark golden retriever right beside the bed, his ears back and his demeanor threatening.

Lisa rolled to the side of the bed and stood. "Piper, no. I told you Riley is a friend." She padded across the room and pointed out into the hallway. "Go."

The dog looked from his mistress to the man threatening his home, obviously confused.

"Piper. Go," she commanded.

The dog padded out and she closed the door, then returned to lie beside Riley.

A touch of amusement tilted the corners of her mouth, but her eyes were still filled with sultry passion. "I don't know what's wrong with him. Dogs are usually such good judges of character."

"Maybe he doesn't want to share your affections."

She tucked her hair behind her ear and asked, "You think I feel affection for you?"

Taking her in his arms, he outlined her lips with a finger, kissed the corner of her mouth and studied her features. "No, I just hope you do."

She'd told him they'd met years ago in school, but he only vaguely remembered the girl she'd been then. The fact that they'd met before explained the sense of déjà vu he'd experienced the evening they'd examined the wine list together, though. It was the way she'd told him that disturbed him. And the timing.

She'd said it the night after they'd made love as he'd dropped her off at her house, almost like a "so there" parting shot. She'd never mentioned it again.

"You're still just appreciating the view," she said. "Piper didn't spoil the mood, did he?"

"I like to look. The same way you like to say my name." He thought she blushed.

"Go ahead. Say it."

"No, you can't make me now."

"I'll bet I can."

"You're on."

She said his name a dozen times with as many inflections over the next hour. He loved his name on her lips, loved her hair, adored the sounds she made when he brought her pleasure. He even loved her creaky bed.

Spent, Riley lay on his back, his skin damp with perspiration, and felt her heartbeat against his ribs. She drew lazy circles in the hair on his belly with one finger. He loved everything about being with Lisa Martin.

And he wanted to tell her.

"Lisa."

"Hmm?"

"I love you."

Her finger stilled. The sound of her ticking alarm clock filled his ears. He shouldn't have said it. He shouldn't have thought it. What had he expected her to do? Return the sentiment?

Initially yes, he had. He'd thought it would be an easy task to ingratiate himself and make himself invaluable. He hadn't planned to feel anything. He hadn't planned to care. Hadn't planned to mean it.

"I have a feeling that you've loved a lot of women," she said at last, her tone light.

He bit back an argument.

"Like you love your Jag and you love blackened steak a little rare. Like you love a really good vintage wine."

He didn't say anything, but his heart hammered.

She scooted upward on the bed with a creak of metal and sat with the sheets held against her breasts. The hair at her temples had turned to corkscrews.

"Tell me that's what you meant, Riley, because I don't want anything to happen to our relationship. We have to see each other at meetings, and you're contracted as my advisor. What we've already done is probably unwise and unprofessional…but I don't want it to be a big mistake."

He managed an easy smile that he didn't feel. "Of course that's what I meant. Actually you're better than wine, but my Jag? I'll need more time to think about that."

Lisa eased back against the pillows.

He'd passed off the uncomfortable moment with a stab at humor, and she seemed appeased. He should have his head examined. He should have his tongue glued to the roof of his mouth. He should *not* be letting feelings get in the way.

"Will you show me the way out to the cabin tomorrow?" she asked. "That is, as long as it's still okay for me to stay there for a while."

"Of course it is. Let me know when you're ready."

"I've had a couple of calls for interviews since the *People* thing. Did you see it?"

"Marge showed me. Are you accepting them?"

"No. I really just want this to blow over. I don't want to be on television."

"Maybe one big interview would satisfy the curiosity."

"That's what we thought about the locals, too."

"Your picture hasn't been in the *Nugget* for a couple of days now."

She picked at a thread on her bedspread. "I'll think about it."

"Lisa, did we graduate together?"

"No, I was a sophomore when you were a senior."

"A sophomore coaching me with chemistry? That hurts."

"A young sophomore, too," she added with a grin. "I skipped a grade in elementary school."

"Double ouch. Do you have any yearbooks?"

"Somewhere."

"Can I look at them?"

She got up and opened her closet, where she snagged a thick chenille robe and pulled it on. Then she pushed aside clothing and pulled out a couple of boxes. Inside the second one she found three volumes of the Thunder Canyon High yearbook and carried them back to the bed.

Riley reached for the lamp on the night table and switched it on before sitting back against the piled pillows.

"What do you want to see?" she asked, laying the books beside him.

"You."

"Oh, come on." She reached to take back the books, but he spread his hand on the top one and held the pile fast.

He glanced at the dates and covers and recalled having one the same. The volume was from the year he graduated. Opening it, he saw none of the youthful writings and scribbled good wishes that littered the pages of his. He quickly found *Martin, Lisa J.* in the directory and noted the three pages where her picture would be found.

In the first snapshot, sixteen members of the chess club smiled for the camera. He scanned the faces without recognition, then read the names listed below and found her. The same wild hair she'd had only a month ago, a concealing sweater and long skirt.

The second picture showed the library volunteers gathered around a display of presidential biographies. He picked her out this time, noting her shy expression and the way she stood behind someone else's shoulder.

"Which one has your graduation picture?"

"You've already seen it on TV."

"I'll find it myself."

"That one."

He opened the book she'd indicated and located her picture. Yes, he'd seen the picture on the news, but he hadn't known then that they'd met before. He studied the photo now.

Like a blurry image coming into focus, memories of Lisa watching him in the cafeteria, on the football field, in the library became clear. This was the quiet girl who had tutored him? He'd like to think he'd been too focused on learning the concepts and passing the class to get to know her. As the memories returned, the sting of conscience bit him.

"You worked in the cafeteria."

"Yes."

How had he not noticed her? Had he been that busy? That full of himself? So caught up in his social activities that a sophomore outside his circle was invisible?

"Don't try to figure it out," she said, as though reading his mind. "I worked at not being seen."

"Why?"

She shrugged. "A lot of reasons. The Lily thing was part of it—not wanting to draw attention. I didn't have clothes that were in style or hair like the other girls. I just didn't fit in and eventually it became my identity."

Lisa blushed and looked away as though she'd revealed too much of herself.

"And now? Who are you now?"

She took the yearbooks and moved them to the night table. "I'm not ashamed of Lily anymore. And I guess I can have all the clothes I want, huh?"

"What about guys? Boyfriends?"

"I can have all of those I want, too, huh?"

She'd deliberately sidestepped his question, not to mention implied that he wasn't her only option. The insinuation made a fist of anger rise in his chest. Anger. Possessiveness. Things he shouldn't be feeling. He had something to ask her and he was going to have to ask soon.

Her reaction to his hastily spoken declaration had been his warning to tread softly, however. The last thing he wanted to do was scare her off. This wasn't a sure thing yet.

"I'll just have to prove I'm enough." He slid a hand inside the robe and stroked the warm, soft skin of her waist and hip. "Think it'll take much convincing tonight?"

"Definitely. I've been having recurring thoughts of Orlando Bloom."

"Who?"

"Never mind. Convince me."

Riley was so large, he took up more than half the space in the bed. She woke in the dark with her body conformed to his. A glance at the luminous dial on her clock told her it was only a little after four. Lisa had never slept beside a man. She'd never shared a bed with anyone except her dogs, and the thought of them being closed out of the room gave her a twinge of guilt. She couldn't let them in now, not with Riley in the bed.

Getting up, she found her robe on the floor and tip-toed to the door. Piper lay in the hall as though guarding her room. At her exit, he scrambled to his feet. She pulled the door shut behind her, not risking the chance of another confrontation.

"Hey, boy." She bent to pet him before moving on down the hall and descending the steps.

Joey had been sleeping on the pile of blankets beside the sofa, and she told him what a good dog he was for sparing her furniture. Both dogs padded behind her into the kitchen.

She poured fresh water into their bowls and got herself a glass of milk. "Hope you're not taking this personally." She sipped her milk and glanced at their accusatory expressions. "I know having him here is out of the ordinary. But there's a lot to be said for new experiences. Ordinary can really suck."

Joey lay down with his chin on his front paws and blinked up at her. Piper glanced toward the doorway, as if he knew who she was talking about and didn't like being kicked to the curb one bit.

"It's not forever, guys, trust me. Please don't begrudge me this one thing for as long as it lasts. I had to know. I had to do something for me just this once."

Plumbing in the upstairs recesses of the house clanged. He was awake.

"C'mon, boys, outside."

They scrambled to the back door, which she unlocked before ushering them out.

"What are you doing up so early?" Riley entered the kitchen wearing his black trousers and carrying his shirt and shoes. His dark hair was endearingly messy.

"I just woke up."

He set the clothes on the seat of a chair. "I guess I'll head out."

"Want to stay for breakfast?"

"I couldn't eat this early. And I should be out of here before daylight." He slipped on the wrinkled shirt.

"Okay." She leaned back against the counter. "I'll pack a few things, buy groceries and be ready to go by this afternoon."

"Why don't you just drive out to my place when you're ready? I'll show you the way from there."

She was planning to spend time alone and knew better than to add complications, but she found herself asking, "Will you stay to have dinner with me tonight?"

A smile creased his cheeks as he sat to pull on his socks and shoes. "I'll do you one better. I'll help you fix it."

Lisa stepped forward and cradled his head against her breast. Riley wrapped his arms around her hips and hugged her tight.

She backed away then and he stood, finding his suit coat and fishing in his pocket for his keys. She walked him to the front door and stood watching as he headed down her street on foot in the dark. Several minutes later she was still watching from between the parted lace on the front windows when his Jaguar rolled by slowly. The taillights disappeared in the darkness.

Lisa was beginning to frighten herself with the thoughts and feelings she had difficulty controlling. The fact that Riley was pursuing her for the gold mine and that she was only turning the tables on him for her own satisfaction was getting harder and harder to remember.

He'd been her first crush, and as that had existed only in fantasy and dreams. All these years later he'd become her first lover. And the reality—the *physicality* of the man—was becoming her undoing. Physical pleasure and blooming friendship had combined with her new self-confidence to fling all those years of loneliness and emptiness in her face.

She didn't want to let go.

She didn't have to just yet.

She hadn't wanted him to move things forward, hadn't allowed him to take his scheme to another level. When he'd mentioned love, her foolish heart had wanted to hear the words, but her sensible head had warned her it meant the end. As soon as he made a move she couldn't counter, she would have to end this.

Originally, selfishly, she hadn't thought past that

first night. But after she'd made love with Riley—
after it looked like the game could continue a little
longer—she'd had to rethink her strategy and
strengthen her defenses.

The deception felt wrong, but she justified her actions with the fact that he'd been the first to deceive.
She'd been staying a step ahead of him all along, but
now it felt as if she had to run to do that.

Lisa let the dogs in and climbed the stairs with them
at her heels. They sniffed every corner of the room as
well as her bed before climbing up beside her where she
lay. She still had a couple of hours before she had to get
up, and now she could sleep without Riley's presence
disturbing her.

She didn't sleep, though. When daylight broke
through her curtains, she was still awake, reliving their
night together and hoping for more time.

Thunder Canyon was more quiet than usual for a
Sunday afternoon, maybe because the sun climbed high
and hot and baked the little town, chasing residents in-
doors. Lisa appreciated it, because no one seemed to pay
her any interest.

Once she had her supplies loaded into the Blazer, she
ushered the dogs into the back and cranked the air-conditioning. She checked the rearview mirror continu-
ously, but no one followed her. She arrived on the Lazy
D and at Riley's home without unwanted attention.

She rang the bell and waited.

Riley opened the door. The T-shirt he wore was
damp with sweat and his face was flushed, his hair

wet. His attention immediately focused on the length of her legs in the first pair of shorts she'd worn since she was a kid. "Wow."

Lisa's cheeks warmed at his appreciative reaction.

He grinned and gestured for her to come in. "I just finished riding and putting up a horse. Can you wait for me to take a quick shower?"

"Sure. I have to bring in the dogs out of the car." She led them in on leashes and cautioned Piper when he growled at Riley.

"Living room's that way. Make yourself at home. I'll be right back."

She ushered the dogs into the room he indicated. Sleek modern sofas and chairs, nickel-finish tables with glass tops and track lighting defined the room. Everything was plain and cold looking. "You guys would have to shed…and we'd need some real furniture to feel at home, wouldn't we?"

The dogs sniffed around, apparently finding nothing of interest because they just sat and panted.

Lisa tested a chair and then the sofa. "Not so bad, really, if a person didn't want somewhere to rest their arms." None of the pieces had armrests. "Probably cost a fortune, too, if I know Riley's taste."

True to his word, Riley returned in a matter of minutes, smelling like soap. His black hair was damp and combed into place. "Ready?"

Piper stood and growled.

"Sorry," Lisa said.

"It's not as big of a deal today, now that I have my pants on," he told her.

She ignored that comment. "Does this stuff really reflect you? Or do you have a decorator?"

He glanced around, seeming a little surprised at her question. "Well...I did have a decorator."

"For some reason I feel a little better about that."

He gave her a look that said he thought she was a fry short of a Happy Meal before turning away. "I have to get something from the kitchen."

She took the dogs outside ahead of him and loaded them back into the Blazer. Riley carried a small cooler out to his Jag.

Getting to his cabin took a little over a half hour, and she tried to remember the landmarks along the way so she could find the place on her own again—or so she could leave and return.

She parked in the double garage beside Riley and he led the way up the stairs. "Don't let that dog get too close," he called over his shoulder.

"I'm watching your butt," she replied.

"I know, just don't let that dog get too close."

"I don't know why he growls at you."

"He's going to like me tonight."

"Why do you say that?"

"Because I'm good at convincing."

She couldn't argue with that. She hadn't had a thought about Orlando Bloom all day.

After being released from their leashes, the dogs checked out every room.

"Do I have to take them down through the garage to do their business every time?"

"No, look here." He showed her into an enormous

suite where double glass doors led to a balcony. "You can use any room you like, but this side of the house is set against a hill. Those stairs lead up to the top, where there's a wooded area and a great view. C'mon, I'll show you."

Lisa called and the animals tagged after them.

Riley took the stairs first and Lisa followed. The dogs took some coaxing, but Piper came first and then Joey.

They came out on a flat expanse of land surrounded by woods and a sharp decline on one side.

"Can anyone get to the house this way?"

"No, it's too high above the roads and there's no path except deer trails. You're safe here."

"What about wild animals?"

"I'm sure there are some, so stay close to the steps if you have to come out at night. There's a flashlight beside the sliding doors. There's a cell phone plugged in on the kitchen counter, too."

Piper and Joey had taken off into the underbrush and returned with leaves clinging to their fur. She knelt and cleaned them off.

Joey brushed up against Riley, pausing to sit at his feet.

Riley scratched the retriever's head. "This looks like a fun hangout, doesn't it? Wait till you see what I have planned for supper."

After that they made several trips with Lisa's belongings and the groceries. Riley carried in the cooler and took out steaks and a familiar white take-out box.

"What's that?" she asked.

"That's *your* bribe. The steak is theirs."

"It's chocolate-raspberry truffle, isn't it?" She reached for the box.

He caught her hand and wrapped her arm around his waist. Lowering his face to hers, he said, "You don't want dessert first, do you?"

"Is that a trick question?"

He kissed her, and she leaned into the embrace.

From the other side of the room, Piper growled.

She started to say something, but Riley stopped her. "Don't worry. Tonight we're going to make friends."

He'd purchased three thick T-bone steaks, one for each of them and one for the dogs to share. "Don't tell me you don't feed them table food," he said. "It's just this once."

"Oh, I don't feed them table food," she pointed out. "Pizza and beer don't count. They're TV cuisine."

It only took Piper thirty seconds to warm to the offering Riley fed him in bite-size pieces as they sat on the deck and enjoyed the sunset. By the time his half of the steak was history, Piper was putty in Riley's hands. He licked his chops, then Riley's fingers, and burped.

"Same effect I have on you," Riley told her.

She took another blissful bite of her chocolate truffle and didn't argue. She did, however, resist burping.

They cleared away dishes and Lisa took the dogs up top to do their business while Riley lit citronella candles and opened a bottle of wine.

"You're going to turn me into a lush," she told him. But she accepted the glass and sipped.

"Do I need to lock my wine cellar while you're staying here?"

"Probably."

He grinned and pulled his canvas chair close to hers.

Piper propped his head on Riley's feet and groaned an exhausted sigh. She knew the feeling. The man had the ability to wear down the fiercest opponent.

"Is this how you negotiate business deals, as well?" she asked.

"Sometimes."

She'd seen the food and drinks offered for business meetings, so the suggestion wasn't far off.

Within minutes Lisa had moved to sit on his lap. Leisurely kisses turned hot and hungry, and she threaded her fingers into his hair.

"Lisa…" he said against her mouth.

She worked her fingers under the hem of his knit shirt and splayed her palm over his chest. "The answer is yes."

"You'd better hear the question first."

She smiled and tasted his mouth once more. This would be good. Anticipation shot through her nerve endings. Just being here where they'd first made love got her hot. He was going to invite her inside, maybe ask her to take off her clothes…suggest something exciting and erotic. "Ask away."

He touched her through her shorts and heat reached through the layer of fabric to make her squirm. He took his mouth from hers, pierced her with intense blue eyes and asked, "Will you marry me?"

Chapter Eleven

It took thirty seconds for Lisa's brain to catch up. When it did, a sinking rush of disappointment flooded through her chest and tears stung her eyes. To hide them she tucked her head under his chin and grabbed the front of his shirt. He'd done it. He'd moved so far out ahead of her, she wouldn't be able to catch up.

Her body still hummed with desire, but her heart and head had started erecting barriers. She struggled to find something sophisticated and witty to say, something that would diffuse the tension and leave them with the basics of their relationship intact. Nothing came to her. Nothing but a crushing sense of defeat.

"Why would we want to spoil a perfectly good thing?" she asked finally. "I mean, we have the best of everything right now, wouldn't you say? I'm not much at compromising, and you wouldn't want to share my lifestyle any more than I'd want to share yours."

"What are you talking about?" he asked.

Once again in control of her emotions, she straightened on his lap. "Think about it. Where would we live?"

"Does it matter?"

"Well, yes, it matters. My house isn't your style, and your house certainly isn't my style."

"You aren't planning to stay in that house, are you?"

"Why not?"

"Lisa, you're—" He cut himself off.

"A millionaire," she finished. "Rich. Yes, so I keep hearing. And so there must be something wrong with my home since I can afford better."

He shrugged. "I just assumed you'd build one."

"Because that's what you would do, Riley."

"We could build a home together. One that suits us both."

"It's foolish to talk about houses. It's foolish to talk about anything that permanent. What's the big rush, anyway? Things were going just fine." She pushed away and stood, walking to the railing and standing with a hand on a support beam.

"It didn't seem like such a bad idea to me."

Of course not—all his ideas were pure genius. "You don't need me. You were doing perfectly well before we met and you'll do just as well after—after this time together is over."

Ever since her ownership of the Queen of Hearts had been discovered, she'd felt as if she was being rushed and pushed in directions she wasn't prepared to go. The fact that she'd suspected Riley's true intent from the beginning didn't make it any easier to accept now that he'd brought his design out in the open.

"I was hoping we could take things to another level," he said, rising and coming to stand behind her.

"Why?"

He placed his hands on her upper arms and turned her to face him. "Why do most people get married?"

"We're not most people, though, are we?"

"I'm sorry for jumping ahead, Lisa. If you need more time, I'm okay with that. Just don't say no."

He lowered his head, and she was too foolish to turn away. She wanted this time with him, even if it would be their last. Raising a hand to his cheek, she returned his kiss.

Time wasn't going to fix this. Time wasn't going to wipe out her knowledge and make this sham real.

"Why don't we just concentrate on tonight?" she said finally.

If their kisses seemed tinged with desperation, she was the one responsible. If there was a sadness and finality to their lovemaking that night, it was because she had said goodbye in her heart.

They were more subdued, and fewer words were spoken between them than on the previous night. And even though no prying eyes would be there to see him leave in the morning, she didn't want to fall asleep beside him or wake by his side. She didn't want ownership of any more memories than those they'd already created.

Once he slept, she crept from his room down to the suite. She urged Joey and Piper up onto the bed with her, fighting the urge to take the boys and escape back to her own house. She had to stand her ground. She had to convince herself she could go back to life before Riley.

Lisa woke early to the smell of coffee wafting through the cabin. She let the dogs out and gave them time to run around the wooded area before calling them back in.

She found coffee in the pot on the counter and then located Riley on the front balcony. He had already shaved, showered and dressed in clothes for work. She joined him and studied the view. In full daylight the scene was indeed as breathtaking as he'd predicted.

"Sleep well?" he asked.

She glanced at him, sensing the new awkwardness between them. "I did. I see you're ready for the day."

He nodded. "I have a meeting with Justin this morning."

She looked at him curiously.

"He's involved with the resort."

"Oh. I wasn't aware of that."

He sipped his coffee. "You should have everything here that you need."

They were quiet for a moment, then Lisa broke the silence.

"I want to say something."

He turned and studied her. "Go ahead."

"I think from here on out we should keep things between us...professional."

Only the twitch in his jaw revealed any reaction.

"If you want to take back your invitation for us to stay here, I'd understand. I don't want to take advantage of you."

A look of discomfort crossed his features at her words. "Of course I don't want to take it back. You're perfectly welcome to stay here."

"Things just went a little too far, Riley. We had a good time. Let's leave it at that."

"A good time," he said, his voice flat.

"A *very* good time," she stressed.

His piercing green gaze flickered over the nearby woods, then back to her face. "I should probably forewarn you. I'm persistent."

"Your persistence won't do you any good this time."

"Persuasive, as well."

"I know."

She could tell there was an argument on his tongue, but to his credit, he held it.

"I'll call the cell number if I see any interesting news clips or if anything comes up," he said.

She nodded with a smile. "I'll answer."

There was a clumsy pause before he carried his cup into the cabin. Lisa followed in time to see him bend to pet each of the dogs. Picking up his sport jacket, he headed for the stairs.

She refilled her cup and observed from the balcony, as below, his bright red Jaguar could be seen through the trees until he'd roared out of sight and beyond hearing range.

She remained on the balcony until hunger drove her in to find something for breakfast.

Her well-planned getaway had lost a lot of its appeal overnight. She'd been alone with animals for companions her whole life and now here she was again. She'd made a huge effort to change herself inside and out and she'd done a damned fine job of it. Problem was she'd hooked herself up with someone she couldn't trust and whose friendship—or whatever it was—was only temporary.

But she wasn't going to worry or pine away her vacation time. She was going to rest, read, walk in the woods and go back to Thunder Canyon refreshed next week. Lisa set about that plan with renewed determination.

She spoke with Bernadine several times over the next few days. Occasionally she used the cell phone to call clients and double-check on her pets. Riley called twice regarding business decisions, three times about some trivial mention of her in the newspaper and once every evening just to ask how she was doing.

She missed him so much, she was tempted to ask him to join her, but she resisted the impulse. The lure, however, was too much when he called her Friday morning and mentioned he'd like to drive out the following night and bring dinner.

"I've missed you," he said, and his voice sent shivers along her nerve endings and made her nipples tighten. "I promise to keep things light. We'll just enjoy being together. Okay?"

Who was she kidding? She didn't have any resistance when it came to this man. She'd dreamed about him each night and thought about him every waking hour. How could she not when she was staying in his cabin?

"I'll bring dessert," he suggested.

That was low.

"Chocolate raspberry truffle."

She caved. "Okay."

That afternoon she took a long soak in the enormous whirlpool tub, thinking about the following night and smiling to herself because she'd brought along a couple of sexy new sundresses. She'd try one out on Riley.

After drying off and taking time to apply scented body lotion and paint her nails, she dressed in a pair of soft lounging pajamas and padded out to the kitchen to make popcorn. Riley didn't own a VCR or a DVD player, but she'd packed several books. The balcony was well shaded this time of day, and she was coming to enjoy the sounds of nature and the fresh air.

The cell phone on the counter beeped, so she checked it while the microwave ticked the minutes backward and the mouthwatering smell of butter filled the room. Maybe Riley was impatient and wanted to drive out sooner. It took her a few minutes to figure out which buttons to push, but she finally retrieved the message. The number on the digital display didn't mean anything to her, so she listened to the recording.

"Riley, where in blazes are you?" The voice belonged to Caleb, and he sounded perturbed. She should probably call Riley and tell him his father was looking for him.

"You dodged our meeting deliberately, didn't you? I'm starting to wonder what you're up to. What is taking so long for you to win over the dog walker? You losing your touch?"

Popcorn popped in the background, but Lisa's attention was riveted on the message meant for Riley.

"It shouldn't be that difficult, son. She's a nobody, and you're a Douglas. Charm her. Get into her pants— hell, knock her up if you have to. Just get a ring on her finger."

Numbness spread across Lisa's scalp in a horrifying confirmation. She'd known. She'd guessed from the very beginning. She wasn't stupid. But hearing the plan so crudely outlined was like rubbing salt in a fresh wound.

"The mine is producing," the recording of Caleb was saying, *"and where are we? Sitting with our thumbs up our asses, that's where. Don't avoid me, I don't like it. And don't waste any more time. I like that even less."*

The message ended with a click and a beep. Lisa stared at the phone before collecting herself enough to locate the off button and press it. She placed the handset back on the charger.

She's a nobody and you're a Douglas. That statement clanged around in her head for several jagged minutes. It was the truth. But as was the case more often than not, the truth hurt. Like hell in this instance.

Caleb had just confirmed what she'd known in her heart all along. She'd had Riley tagged the minute he'd shown an interest—before she'd transformed herself. Riley wasn't any better than the so-called cousins who'd been calling.

The fact that his father had been in on the plan all along cheapened what they'd done all the more, though. Had Riley gone back and reported to his father each time they'd been together? How sleazy did that make her feel?

She'd felt so smug in her ability to be the seductress and to turn the tables on him. She'd only been kidding herself that she was in control.

"You knew," she told herself. "This isn't a big revelation. You had his number from the beginning and you chose to play along. It's not like you've been tricked into thinking he loves you."

She took the popcorn from the microwave, grabbed her book and went out to the balcony. Joey and Piper followed and begged at her feet. She shoved Caleb's angry voice and superior tone out of her head and forced her eyes to the pages.

An hour later the two retrievers licked up the last of the popcorn from where the bag had fallen, and Lisa stared out across the wooded landscape. Dozens of plans formed in her head. Scenarios where she told off Riley in glorious eloquence. Scenes in which she won his undying love and devotion.

Should she still let him come to the cabin tomorrow night? Should she behave as though she hadn't heard the message? Or should she confront him now—call him this minute—and get the truth out in the open and over with? Or…she could be gone when he got here. She could take an extended trip and not tell him where she'd gone.

She could go someplace where people didn't know her or recognize her and see if she couldn't find a man who would be attracted to her *for her,* not for her gold mine.

What she could not do was be unprepared. Drift. Waver. She'd made up her mind to cool things off, then she'd gone and let him talk her into another night.

Get an upper hand, that's what she had to do.

Lisa went into the house and used the phone to make dinner reservations for the following evening. Then she called Riley's cell phone.

He answered, "Hey, Lisa."

He must have this number programmed into his phone. She wasn't savvy about this technical stuff, but she was figuring it out. "Uh, hi."

"What's up?"

"Change of plans. I made reservations at the Blue Moon in Billings for tomorrow evening. Meet me there at seven."

"Coming back early or just going out for dinner?" His voice brought back sensual memories. It probably always would.

"I'm heading back early. I've relaxed enough. I'm out of books and popcorn."

He chuckled. "Okay. You'll find your way back okay?"

"No problem. See you then."

Lisa had lain awake for hours trying to think of the very thing that would set Riley on his ear and show him she wasn't a puppet. The only fitting plan she could come up with was another man.

One small problem: there was no other man. Not that she couldn't find one. Offers came in daily, if her mailbox was any indicator. But for the most impact, it couldn't be just any man. It had to be one Riley would see as a true threat.

The next day she drove to Thunder Canyon and shopped for groceries before driving home. The house welcomed her like an old friend. She walked through the rooms comforted by the familiarity. The dogs seemed glad to be back, as well, dozing in a patch of sunlight that streamed through the dining room windows while she dusted and vacuumed.

Lisa sat with a glass of iced tea and read through piles of mail looking for something suitable, searching for just the right catalyst.

Finally she found him.

Phil Wagner. A formal letter with his business card almost scorched her hands. He wasn't married, was he? She didn't recall anyone accompanying him at the Douglases' party, but it would be easy enough to find out.

She needed a financial advisor, and Riley had recommended this guy. It was Saturday, but she took a chance and called him anyway. She left a message, mentioned she'd just returned to find his letter and would like to talk.

Fifteen minutes later, as she was putting away her clothing and toiletries, the phone rang.

"Phil Wagner here. I got your message."

"Thanks for calling back so quickly."

"No problem. What can I do for you?"

"I was wondering if it was too late and you already had plans for this evening. Riley and I are having dinner, and I was hoping you could join us. Your wife is welcome to join us, of course."

He chuckled. "I'm not married."

"Oh. Well, a date, then."

"I try not to mix business and pleasure."

"Probably a wise philosophy," she replied. "It's

really last-minute, so I'd understand if you can't make it."

"I can make it," he said after a second. "Give me the details."

"Can I pick you up around six thirty?"

"Sure." He gave her his address and she hung up.

For half an hour she fought down a rush of panic and guilt. After that passed she told herself there was no guarantee that Phil would even be attracted to her. He didn't have to —all he had to do was show up with her.

She took a few antacids and sat at the kitchen table. What a laughable creature she was. Her money would do any attracting that needed done—a sad fact to look forward to for the rest of her life.

Phil's his friend. You're playing with fire. You're playing dirty.

Oh? And what had Riley done? Played fair?

Two wrongs don't make a right.

No, but this one will sure be fun.

Revenge is not sweet; it's wrong.

This wasn't revenge. It was…turnabout. And turnabout was fair play. As long as her conscience was going to throw every cliché in the book at her, she was going to counter with a few, as well.

Her nails were already done, and she took her time straightening and styling her hair and applying makeup. She dressed in pale silver pants with a matching spaghetti-strap top and draped a sheer black shawl around her shoulders. It reminded her of the gauzy black fabric that draped over Lily Divine's hip in the painting at the Hitching Post.

Lily had been a self-made woman, a woman proud of

her accomplishments. What would she think if she knew the Queen of Hearts was producing gold and making Lisa rich? How would she see Lisa's actions? Apparently Lily had dealt with an overbearing Douglas, as well, so hopefully she'd be delighted to know Lisa wasn't letting the present-day Douglases get the best of her.

Lisa swallowed down her anxiety on the drive to Phil's. He lived in a nice condo in New Town, and she didn't have any trouble finding it. He was dressed in a pair of black slacks and a gray suit jacket and he greeted her with a smile.

"This is a nice change of pace," he said. "Going out to dinner with a pretty lady rather than a bunch of men."

"I learned from Riley that you wine and dine the people you want to impress," she said lightly.

He laughed. "Impress or coerce?"

Phil was nice looking in a young Jeff Daniels sort of way. There was nothing threatening or intimidating about him, and she didn't sense a superior attitude. He was just plain nice, and she wondered what he and Riley had in common.

"Just out of curiosity, what kind of car do you drive?" she asked.

"Business or pleasure?"

Okay, there was one similarity. "Both."

"I have a nice, sensible Camry. Silver."

"And for pleasure?"

"A black Chevy pickup with a bright red front bumper and red flames painted up the sides."

"I've seen it." A vehicle that flashy was hard to miss. He asked her about the recent goings-on with the mine, and as they got closer to their destination she explained several details about the initial extraction.

"Sounds like you've learned the business," he said as she pulled into the parking lot at the Blue Moon restaurant.

"I'm determined to keep up," she told him.

They got out and met in front of the Blazer. Lisa led the way in, glancing at her watch. Her stomach dipped in anticipation of what was to come.

Inside, a hostess directed them to a table where Riley was seated. The expression on his face when he saw the two of them was a priceless combination of surprise and confusion. Being the Douglas he was, however, he quickly masked his bewilderment and greeted both of them as though he'd known this was the plan all along. He stood, but Phil was already pulling out Lisa's chair.

Lisa sat and gave Riley a friendly smile while Phil took a seat on her other side.

With an envious look the hostess handed each of them a menu and inquired what they'd like to drink. "I'd like a bottle of wine, but Mr. Douglas will select it," Lisa said to the young woman.

Riley ordered a vintage cabernet, and the hostess left with a nod.

Lisa almost laughed at the absurdity of the situation. A month ago she'd never even been in a restaurant this nice, had never been seen with one handsome man, and now she was seated here with two.

"You seem in a good mood this evening," Riley commented. "Your vacation must have been refreshing."

"That's right, you mentioned you'd just returned home," Phil said. "Where'd you go?"

"A little getaway place you might know of," she replied. "Riley said you use the cabin occasionally."

"Riley's so-called cabin? It has more amenities than my condo. I'd been thinking I needed a retreat of my own, but he went to so much work, and the place is used so seldom, I figure why not take him up on his offer to use it."

"My boys loved it," she said. Then explained, "Three- and four-year-old golden retrievers."

"I've seen them with you in the photographs. They're beauties. I have a black Lab myself. He's almost five. I got him when he was six months old."

"What's his name?"

"MacGuyver. He'd been abused and was untrusting. Wouldn't even eat if I was in the room."

"Poor guy. He adjusted to you and your home, though?"

"Oh, yeah. Occasionally if I talk loud or shout—like during a Seahawks game—he starts shaking and tries to hide. But I just coax him out of it, and he's fine. He's a big baby, really. Sleeps on my sofa while I'm at work."

"Joey and Piper aren't allowed on the sofa, but they sleep with me at night. And I only have a full-size bed."

"Must be a little crowded."

Lisa chuckled and glanced at Riley. His jaw muscle was working so hard, he looked as if he could bite through the steel table leg.

Their server arrived with the bottle of wine, and Lisa gestured for her to have Riley taste it.

"It's fine," he told her, and she poured.

"Well," Lisa said, extending her glass. "To pleasant and profitable business transactions and to new friends."

The two men raised their glasses and they drank.

Phil steered the conversation to his investment suggestions, and Lisa listened with fascination. Occasionally Riley disagreed or had an alternative suggestion, but all in all the two men agreed on a plan for Lisa's venture capital.

At one point as she listened, her attention wavered to Riley and her thoughts drifted to the intimacies they'd shared.

Charm her. Get into her pants—hell, knock her up if you have to. Just get a ring on her finger.

Oh, he'd charmed her. More than that, he'd swept her off her ever-lovin' feet. As for getting into her pants, well, that had been mutual—she'd accessed his pants just as eagerly.

Knocked up? He'd wisely and safely used a condom each time they'd been together. At least he hadn't stooped that low—not that she'd have let him. She'd been hot, not stupid.

He'd suggested the ring. He'd gone beyond that, though, gone above and beyond his father's demands and professed love.

Looking at Riley now, Lisa wanted to cry.

She excused herself and found the ladies' room. She had no basis for self-pity, no grounds for feelings of betrayal. She'd been a willing participant from the get-go. And she'd known all along that he was deceiving her.

She hadn't just gone along with him. No, she'd initiated and prompted and used his determination for her own purposes. Lisa washed her hands and touched up her lipstick before heading back to the table.

The server brought their meals, and she ate her wild rice and salmon with an uncharacteristic lack of fervor. Even the wine lost its appeal and she declined a refill.

They talked a while after their dishes had been cleared. Lisa ordered slices of pie for the men and a dish of sherbet for herself. When the check came, she gave the woman her credit card and signed for their dinner.

Phil had been invited to a business dinner and seemed to take her payment of the bill for granted. Riley, on the other hand, looked decidedly uncomfortable.

Out of doors, the warm summer air skimmed Lisa's skin. She hadn't realized how cool it had been in the restaurant until she noticed how good this felt.

Phil reached to shake Riley's hand. "Thanks for hooking me up, buddy. I'll do a good job for Lisa."

Riley nodded, then glanced at her.

"Good night," she said.

She and Phil walked to her Blazer. She used her remote to unlock the doors, and Phil opened the driver's side for her.

Riley turned away, and several seconds later she saw the headlights on his Jaguar turn on. He was ahead of her as she pulled out of the parking lot and drove toward the highway.

His taillights disappeared in the distance, and she couldn't help wondering what he'd been thinking as they'd parted.

Phil talked about his Lab and asked her about Joey and Piper. It was always a joy to share stories with someone who shared her love of dogs, so they talked and laughed until she dropped him off at his condo.

"I'll be in touch, and we'll set up a meeting this week," he told her, sliding out and leaning in the open doorway.

"Sounds good."

He closed the door and Lisa drove away.

She'd shown Riley. She'd brought another man into the picture, but she didn't feel any better. Her plan didn't feel as rewarding as she'd imagined when she'd cooked it up. She didn't have the coldheartedness to actually lead a man on, so this business meeting would have to be enough of a ruse to prove to Riley that she wasn't hard up.

She pulled into her driveway, and her headlights lit the red reflector lights on the rear of a car. The Jag.

Riley was waiting for her.

Chapter Twelve

Oh, crap.

He wasn't going to take her rejection sitting down. Or by going home. Or by being avoided. He was going to confront her head-on.

She parked the Blazer and got out.

Every air conditioner on the block hummed in the summer night. Somewhere in the distance a dog barked.

Out of habit Lisa glanced around, not seeing any news vehicles.

Riley met her on the brick walkway to the house. "What was that all about?"

"What was what all about?"

"You know good and well what. We had a date."

Six nights ago he'd asked her to marry him. Tonight

she'd brought another man to what he'd thought was a date. He was probably a little angry.

"You assumed we had a date. I told you the other day that I wanted things to be professional between us."

"And then we spoke on the phone all week and I asked you out. You accepted."

"Well, I chose to keep things professional."

"So you asked Phil along?"

"He's a nice guy, isn't he?"

"I suppose you stayed to meet his dog."

Why hadn't she thought of that? "Is there some point to this conversation?"

"The point is you brought Phil along to tick me off."

She took her keys out of her handbag and approached her door. Not to tick him off, actually, just to wake him up. "I can have dinner with anyone I like."

Riley followed. "Don't act all innocent. You had an ulterior motive."

She unlocked her door, then turned slowly to face him. "And you'd know all about those, wouldn't you?"

"What are you insinuating?"

"Come on, Riley. I may not have been the best looking or most worldly woman you ever boinked, but I wasn't the stupidest. I remembered *you* from high school, got that? You never gave me a second glance until I inherited a gold mine. Hello?"

Insects buzzed around the light beside her door, so she stepped off the porch onto the sidewalk.

Riley had the grace to momentarily look guilty. "I don't think you're stupid."

"No? Then you think I would really be tricked into

believing you were paying attention to me for myself? I have the pictures, Riley, I know I looked awful."

"You didn't look awful," he denied without much conviction.

She snorted.

"Things just developed between us naturally," he said.

"And the fact that I had just inherited the gold mine you thought belonged to your family *never* had a thing to do with the attraction."

He looked slightly sheepish. "Maybe at first."

"At first? That's bull, and you know it. We both know it. Just stop with the act, will you? Could you just be honest?"

"Lisa, I didn't come here tonight because of the mine. That's honest."

"Really."

"Yes, really."

Behind her the dogs whined and scratched on the inside of the door.

"You might want to retrieve your messages from your other cell phone," she said. "The one at the cabin."

He blinked as though she'd changed the subject. "Why's that?"

"There's an urgent message from your father. Seems you ditched a meeting, and he wasn't very happy with you. He called that number and left an earful."

"What did he say?"

"Oh, he wondered if you were losing your touch since you didn't have a ring on the dog walker's hand yet. He had a few helpful suggestions. Charm her. Get in her pants. Knock her up."

If it had been daylight, she'd probably have seen a new color of green as yet unnamed by Crayola. But as it was, she simply read dismay at having been discovered in the tightening of Riley's lips and his tense stance.

"I have to give you credit, though," she said, gesturing with one hand. "You didn't try the latter suggestion." A flutter of panic battered her chest. "Unless you did something to the condoms beforehand."

"Of course not!" He threaded a hand into his hair and tilted his head back as though praying for deliverance. When at last he looked back at her, he said, "Lisa, I can explain."

"Of course you can. You're a master at getting what you want. It takes a strong person to resist your coercion. A *smart* person."

"May I please explain?"

"Do you deny you had a plan to get into my good graces?"

"No."

"Or that your plan included wining and dining and making me pliable?"

"No."

"Did it ever seem to you that I played along a little too easily?"

"I thought we were connecting."

"Did it ever occur to you that I was giving back to you as good as you were dishing out?"

He swallowed. "Were you?"

"Hello? The whole makeover, the dresses, the… *underwear?*"

"You've been leading *me* on? But…but you were a virgin."

"The word is not a synonym for *ignorant*."

"Lisa, don't you feel something for me?"

An ache swelled in her chest, but she fought it down to salvage her pride. What did he want from her? "Yes, I do feel something," she declared. "Sorry. Because now you have to go tell Daddy your scheme blew up in your face and that there won't be a wedding."

She turned and walked into her house, firmly closing the door and locking it.

Joey and Piper sniffed at her pant legs and licked the hand which still held her keys. She dropped them beside her purse on a table.

A light knock sounded on the door, as though he knew she was still on the other side.

"Lisa, let me in so I can talk to you. Please."

"Go away or I'll call the police and tell them I'm being harassed by a stalker."

He must have taken her threat seriously, because a minute later she heard his car start and saw headlights as he carefully backed out around her Blazer in the drive and left.

Well, there. That was it. She hadn't lost anything because she'd never had anything to lose. Rather, she'd saved her pride and her heart and had an experience she'd wanted in the meantime. No feeling sorry. No turning back. If anything, she'd come out ahead because she'd learned her strengths and discovered her sexuality. She'd held her own against a formidable deceiver.

If all that was true, why did she feel so empty?

"What do you say we go for a run tonight, boys? We're still in reprieve from the media and it's a pretty night."

She could buy a dishwasher. She'd always wanted one.

There really wasn't a place for one, so the cabinets would have to be redone.

Maybe it would be easier to just hire someone to do the dishes. And cook. Not a concept she was comfortable with.

She could buy a new house with a dishwasher and a housekeeper already built in.

Lisa shifted the heavy gold nugget from one hand to the other and set it back on the kitchen table.

The phone rang. She'd bought one with caller ID and had the phone company adjust her service. Riley again. He'd tried to call seven times that morning.

It had been three days since she'd seen him. Three days since she'd told him she was wise to him.

The doorbell rang. The dogs were out back, so they weren't underfoot to bark and trip her on her way to the front hall. Through the leaded-glass door she could see the brown uniform of the delivery man.

"Lisa Martin?"

"That's me."

"Sign here, please." The package he leaned up against the porch wall was six inches thick and about four foot by four foot square.

"Who's it from?"

"Um, Kincaid Restorations?"

"Never heard of them."

"Well, it's for you, miss."

She signed the electronic clipboard and carried the surprisingly heavy box into the house.

She had to get a knife to slice the strapping tape and cut open the end. She slid the packing material out on the floor. Between two thicknesses of foam and several layers of tissue and bubble wrap, she discovered a stained-glass window.

The exquisite piece was Victorian looking but not in a reproduction-type way. It was an antique. The individual pieces of blue, violet and green glass had been intricately leaded to create flowering wisteria and vines.

There was no note, no card, no invoice, and the absence of anything identifying the sender was proof it had been Riley. Who else? And since it had been Riley, that meant the bribe had cost a small fortune.

She couldn't keep it. She'd have to send it back. Or have it delivered to his address.

Lisa leaned the piece of glass up against the leg of a table, and the light from the front windows caught it. Colors spread across the wood floor and the wool rug like an incredible rainbow.

"How much does this suck?" she said to herself. "I get the first gift I've ever had from a man and I can't keep it. And it's really, really beautiful. And he knew I'd love it. The jerk."

Tears came to her eyes, but she blinked them away.

Several things still had to happen. She had to prove to Riley Douglas that she was not a pawn in his game. She had to come to some decisions on what she wanted for herself. And she still wanted to dispel the untruths about Lily.

First things first. Lisa waited until she knew school

would be letting out and drove to the high school. Little had changed since her days there. The outside had been landscaped and a bricked common area created. Inside there were new display cases and the offices had been remodeled to all-window walls.

After checking at the office, she was directed to a second-floor room where Ben Saunders taught.

The man was in his sixties, his hair grayer and his middle thicker than when she'd taken his class. He was putting away books in an oak storage unit at the back of the room.

"Mr. Saunders?"

He blinked and took in her slim skirt and off-the-shoulder pink blouse before smiling. "Lisa Jane! Don't you look just as pretty as all of your pictures. I'm surprised to see you here."

"I wanted to talk to you."

"Well, sure. Have a seat." He pulled out a wooden chair and gestured for her to take it. After she'd seated herself, he brought another and placed it across from her. "What's on your mind?"

"I know you're always involved with Heritage Day and the reenactments of Thunder Canyon history."

"Oh, yes," he replied. "I'm the chairman of the historical society's publicity and ways-and-means committees."

"And several people have mentioned that you're often found at the Hitching Post telling stories about the first gold rush and the early town founders."

He nodded. "There's always a lot of interest in our town history."

"Would you mind telling me the documented facts you know about Lily Divine Harding?" Lisa asked.

"Not at all. She operated the Shady Lady saloon. The operation did a booming business. It was one of three hurdy-gurdy houses in Thunder Canyon."

"Hurdy-gurdy meaning…?"

"Well, that there were women available to dance and, er, entertain the men."

"Do you know of any proof that Lily employed women as prostitutes? Are there letters? Arrests documented?"

He tapped a finger on his chin. "Actually, prostitution wasn't illegal at that time. But there was an organization called the Women's Temperance Prayer League. This group of the town's leading ladies condemned and protested the existence of what they called the 'dens of vice' and had a mission to shut them down. There are a few old meeting flyers in the archives."

"But those only prove that they were accusing the Shady Lady of being a den of vice. Has anything ever proven the fact?"

"Not to my knowledge," he replied.

"I borrowed several journals written by Catherine Douglas from Tildy Matheson."

Ben's eyes lit with excitement. "Emily Stanton—er, Vaughn, I mean—told me those existed."

"Tildy plans to bequeath them to the historical society upon her death."

His expression was intense as he said, "They should be carefully preserved."

"Catherine's things mean a great deal to her. She has treasured them. Catherine makes vague references to

Lily's house being a place of refuge and safety. Tildy's and Emelda Ross's stories back up the fact that Catherine Douglas was abused by her husband and often taken in by Lily."

"I've heard similar stories," he said. "There's a newspaper clip of a Polish woman named Helena who worked in the theater back east before escaping a bad situation with a man and coming to Montana. The article says that Helena found employment and refuge with a local establishment. I've suspected that establishment was the Shady Lady."

"Mr. Saunders, there's no proof that Lily was a prostitute or that her saloon was anything other than a dance hall, is there?"

He shook his head. "The theories have been elaborated over the years because of the painting. And the name of the saloon. It makes for a much more appealing story about the gold-rush days if our Lily was a colorful woman."

"Do you really think it would hurt commerce if the true facts surrounding Lily were made public?"

He shook his head. "I doubt it. After all, we have a present-day gold mine."

"I'd like you to put together all the solid facts regarding Lily, the Shady Lady and anything else relevant, and I'll have a book published for the historical society. You can be the author and take whatever is a fair share for royalties, and the rest of the proceeds will go to the foundation. How does that sound to you?"

His face crinkled with a smile. "It sounds fantastic,

Lisa. I can include photographs and documents from the archives. Perhaps quote from Catherine's journals."

"Okay, then this is your project. If you're aware of presses that do this sort of thing, I'll do the legwork."

"What kind of deadline do you want?" Ben asked.

"We'd like copies in our hands by next Heritage Day, right?" She thought a moment. "How about three or four months?"

"I can do that."

Lisa left the school feeling good about doing all she could to clear up speculation about Lily. They may never have proof of the real story, but at least they could give the facts and let people decide for themselves.

Lisa met Bernadine at the Hitching Post for lunch and told her what she'd come up with.

"That's great, Lisa. That's giving to the community, and they'll love you for it." She glanced at the menu. "What are you getting?"

"I don't know. A hamburger? We need a restaurant as nice as anything in Billings so we don't have to drive all that way for a real meal."

Bernadine laid down her menu. "You're right."

Lisa looked at her. "You really think that's a good idea?"

"I think it's a great idea. If we want to draw tourists to the resort, we'll need some classy places for them to frequent. Besides those on the resort property itself."

"Not anything stuffy, though," Lisa said quickly, getting into the idea with fervor. "Nice decor, maybe tin ceilings for atmosphere. Steaks. Good wine. Fabulous desserts. We'd need a good chef."

"You're getting the hang of this rich-girl stuff," Bernadine told her.

"It could be called the Claim Jumper. We could hang mining memorabilia, old photographs in keeping with the theme of the town and Heritage Days."

"You're really good at this."

"Dog Walker Turned Entrepreneur," Lisa said. "Notice how I think in headlines these days?"

"This is the kind of thing Riley mentioned," Bernadine told her, "when he recommended you put money into local ventures. He'll love this idea."

Lisa wasn't so sure Riley would appreciate anything coming from her right at the moment, but they were going to have to get past their...difficulties...and get down to business.

"I'd love to see his reaction," the other woman added.

"Yeah, I can't wait." Maybe this was it. Maybe this was how she'd show him she had her own mind and her own ideas and didn't intend to be pressured into other people's.

Lisa thought about the women in the movies with men troubles who always confided in their best friends. She didn't have a best friend. Bernadine was her friendly lawyer, but even if she was a friend, she certainly wouldn't have any experience that would benefit Lisa in her bizarre situation.

A confidant was an appealing notion at the moment, however.

A man stopped beside their booth just then, and Lisa glanced up to find Phil Wagner wearing an amiable smile.

"Hi, ladies."

"Hi, Phil," they echoed one after the other.

"I hear you're bringing gold out of the mine this week."

"Yep. Hope you're ready to make money for me."

"I'm ready. I've drawn up a five-year plan to go over with you whenever you have the time."

"I'll have the time this week."

Phil slid a PDA from his pocket and flipped it open. "Thursday looks good in the afternoon. Or Friday morning."

"Any lunches or dinners open?"

"Thursday lunch?"

"Perfect."

"Here?" he asked.

"There's the café and the lunch counter at Super Saver Mart."

"The lunch counter is good," Phil said.

They chose a time, and he moved away to pay his bill and leave.

"Another admirer?" Bernadine asked.

"Another business associate."

"Miss Martin?" Chad Falkner stood beside their booth, no camera in hand.

Lisa glanced around and didn't see any other reporters. "Well. I was wondering when I'd see you."

"Kept our end of the deal, didn't we?"

"Yes, you did."

"Did you see the picture I took in *People?*"

"Oh, yes."

"I was wondering if you have any kind of a follow-up statement to our interview or anything you'd like to share with the public."

Lisa thought a minute. "Actually I do. Have a seat and we'll talk. Have you eaten?"

Chad looked as if he'd been granted an audience with the queen of England. His expression was serious, and he sat beside Lisa with a look of sheer gratification on his face.

"I have a couple of new projects," she told him, "and I'd like people to hear about them from me. One of them is a book on Lily Divine for the historical society. Hopefully it's going to dispel some of the myths that have been perpetuated about her."

"Really?"

Bernadine leaned forward. "There will be press releases regarding Miss Martin's new ventures," she told Chad. "What would you say to seeing those first and hearing any other news she has to share first, as long as you keep your distance the rest of the time? The way you have been."

"I'd say yes. I can try to work out something with the other reporters so that they'll get the same accurate news after I've seen it. You might have to throw them a bone now and then and pose for a few pictures."

"I can do that."

"We'll have something written up for you about this book project next week," Bernadine told him.

"Great. What about the other projects you mentioned? You only told me about one."

"The other one is under wraps for now—at least until some more plans can be made. You'll be the first to know."

He stood and reached to shake both women's hands. "Thanks a lot."

"So, you're my publicist now?" Lisa asked Bernadine.

"No, but I have people who can work up press releases. Anything to keep those bloodsuckers off your tail."

Lisa thanked her and they finally got around to eating their lunch.

She had taken a huge first step toward her goal of clearing Lily's name to the best of her ability. She was handling the press without Riley now and she had come up with her own idea for a local business venture. That should show Riley she had a mind of her own. She still had to figure out what she wanted for herself, though, and that was proving more difficult than the other tasks.

First she'd thought she was happy the way she was and resisted change. Then she'd realized she wanted more and had broken out of her boring shell and tried to change everything about herself at once. She was discovering she was more creative and independent than she'd ever dreamed.

She'd even been enjoying talking to people and coming out of her isolation. Not everyone was out to wheedle a chunk of her gold mine.

"If I didn't have a gold mine anymore," she said offhandedly, "would you still want to have lunch with me?"

Bernadine's expression showed surprised but understanding, as well. "Yes, I would, Lisa. I think we're becoming friends, don't you?"

"Yes, I think so."

The more Lisa thought about it over the next day or so, the more she realized she'd been very judgmental of the townspeople. Sure, there were the crazies who called to convince her they were a long-lost relative, but there were also plenty of other people who were perfectly warm and friendly. She'd always considered that they'd looked down on her and ignored her, but she'd perpetuated that treatment. If she'd stood up to a few juvenile comments in school or had not been ashamed of being related to Lily, maybe things would have been different.

That kind of thinking changed her whole attitude. And scared her. And delighted her. She really had changed.

Riley stood outside Town Hall after a chaotic meeting with officials over the much-needed addition of more police officers, firemen and medical personnel. Ever since the onset of gold fever, the town had been overrun by would-be prospectors and sightseers. Good for the economy but a stretch to their fiscal budgets. The board had asked Riley to head a project to appropriate more dollars for these jobs.

Brad Vaughn paused beside him with a question about additional parking for Main Street shops. Brad and Emily had been married recently and had settled in Thunder Canyon. Brad had started a missing-persons investigation company and he took an active interest in town issues.

"The motels are inadequate for the influx of tourists, as well," Brad told him. "When Emily and I initially arrived here to investigate the mine ownership, we couldn't find anyplace to stay. Your father loaned us that old cabin."

"I heard that was a good thing," Riley replied easily.

"As it turned out, it was, but not everyone has that option. Especially since we bought the place."

"I agree. Even with the resort there will be middle-income tourists looking for an economy stay."

"Emily tells me the Martin girl was reluctant to claim ownership of the mine at first. From what we see in the papers, it looks like she's coming out of her shell now."

"She's come a long way. She wants to learn all she can and manage the monster that was dropped in her lap."

Brad faced Riley with a furrow between his brows. "I hope there's no hard feelings between us now—you know, because Emily and I made the results of our investigation public."

That comment didn't soak in. "What do you mean? You found the only documentation available. It's a legal document. I know we hired you to discover otherwise, but you did find the owner. Why would that create hard feelings?"

Brad gave him an odd look. "Well…" He glanced away. "No reason, I guess."

"No, speak up. In your opinion, why would I resent you?"

Brad seemed hesitant to speak but finally opened up. "When Emily and I found the deed, your father offered us money to keep silent about it being signed back over to Lily Harding. We wouldn't consider it. I thought you knew this."

The information burned in Riley's stomach like three-alarm chili. His father had offered Brad a bribe to keep Lisa's ownership a secret. If left to his own wishes, Caleb would have destroyed the deed and called the mine Douglas property without anyone knowing any different.

Shame heated Riley's flesh. "No. I didn't know. But thank you for your integrity."

"I wasn't sure where you stood," Brad said.

"I haven't been sure most of the time either," Riley replied honestly. "But the lines are becoming a lot more clear."

Brad extended a hand. "No harm done, then?"

"Just the opposite." Riley shook his hand.

He and Brad parted on the sidewalk, and Riley walked toward the street where his car was parked. Family loyalties ran deep, but bribery and deceit were family values he didn't want to condone any longer. He could forgive his father for his acts of adultery, but he had trouble with ignoring the pain his mother had suffered.

The story of Caleb offering Justin's mother money to keep him had always stuck in his craw. Had it made Justin feel valuable?

And now this. Offering the investigators money to hide Lisa's ownership of the mine. Equally as low-down and underhanded as Riley's devising a plan to win her affection and marry her so he could get control, wasn't it? He'd justified his actions by planning to leave her well off when he divorced her. What kind of warped thinking had that been? Why hadn't he rejected the idea when he'd first had it? Because he'd seen all his life how money and power got you what you wanted. What he hadn't seen—or wanted to see—were the far-reaching effects and the slow erosion of virtue when a person allowed this kind of manipulation.

This was the first time he'd admitted these things to himself. He'd never promised his father he would carry out the marriage. But he'd pursued Lisa as though he intended to make it happen.

What could he do to correct such a big, ugly mistake?

She wouldn't even take his calls.

He didn't know how to redeem himself or if it was even possible. But he knew he had to try.

Chapter Thirteen

Every day for the past week Riley had left a message on her machine. Every one-sided conversation had been similar. He wanted to see her. Wanted to talk to her. She was aware of her limitations and knew she was toast if she gave in to him. She would have to get past this and face him for business, but all in good time. For the time being, she checked in with Marge when she had a question or when there was something that needed a signature. Marge accommodated her by using a courier service.

Lisa went about her new life the best way she knew how. And she spent a lot of time thinking about where she wanted to direct her energy and her emotions. Dogs had always been her first love, and caring for them would always be important. Calls for walks and care had dwindled with her rise to local fame, though. Her clients assumed she didn't have the time or the inclination, and truth be told, it was becoming more and more difficult to juggle Puppy Love with her other business obligations.

She still loved her grandmother's house and couldn't imagine not having the security and memories it provided. One evening, out of the blue, the idea came to her that she could move this house to a more suitable location with surrounding land and a security enclosure.

Amazing how money could open doors and move otherwise unoiled gears. Her first phone calls were met by receptive people with the knowledge and skill to help her move the house. Calls to Realtors resulted in appointments to look at property.

Remembering something Emily had said to her the very first day they'd met, Lisa thought about the things she'd always thought she would do if she could afford to. Emily had said she'd pay for her sister's college. Lisa didn't have any siblings, but she'd given a lot of thought to things she would do with her money when she actually had an abundance.

Riley left a message for her to call the bank and verify balances. She did and her ears went numb. She was rich.

He was her financial manager. She needed to clear things with him, so she called Marge and asked her to leave him a message. Previously his secretary had caught on that Lisa didn't want to speak directly to him. Lisa told her she wanted to start a search for property and asked how much she could safely spend this month.

She wanted to implement a plan for an animal shelter, as well. Before she'd understood the magnitude of her inheritance, she'd had it in her heart that building a no-kill facility would be the height of her benevolent dreams. Now there was no reason it couldn't become a reality.

After explaining to Marge, she hung up feeling guilty and called her right back. "Marge, never mind. I'm sorry to have placed you in this position. I'll talk to Riley myself."

"No problem. He's right here."

She had expected him to return her call, not be standing by.

"Hello, Lisa."

"Hi. I want to move on a couple of projects, so I need to run them past you."

"Great. Want me to come over there?"

"We can talk over the phone."

"Whatever makes you happy."

She explained about looking for property and about the animal shelter.

"You'd better hold off on the shelter," he told her.

"Why?"

"You'd be doubling your efforts."

"How so?" she asked. "There's nothing like that in Thunder Canyon."

"But there will be. There's been land purchased."

"By whom?"

He paused only briefly. "By me."

Riley had already bought land for an animal shelter?

"One of the things I need to talk to you about is how to set it up and what features to employ. I thought we could visit a couple in nearby regions and get some ideas."

Lisa had to compose her thoughts to find her tongue. "*You* are planning to build an animal shelter?"

"Yes."

"Why?"

"I heard you mention it once."

"Is this some sort of manipulation technique?"

"No, it's going to be a gift. To the city."

"Why this particular project?"

"Because I know it's close to your heart. And that's where I want to be, as well. I was hoping it would show you I'm not the greedy, scum-sucking control freak you think I am. I admit I got close to fitting that description once, but I'm working at change. I'd like you to take over the project and have the final say on everything."

What did an animal shelter cost? she thought with skepticism. Only a fraction of a gold mine. If he sucked her in with this ploy, he'd still be a cool mil ahead.

"Will you do it?" he asked.

"If you're serious. But not if you think it changes anything."

The line was silent a moment too long. "Will you accept my apology so I can sleep nights?"

Why should he have a sleep advantage over her? "What, a conscience?"

"A conscience, a heart, whatever you want to call it.

I'm sorry. I can't go back and fix it. But I can show you I'm not that same person."

"By building an animal shelter?"

"By doing something I thought you'd respect me for."

"People earn respect, Riley."

"That they do. You earned mine."

She couldn't listen to this. She couldn't weaken. "We're business associates. I don't want to avoid your phone calls. I want to know that when your number shows up, you're calling about business. I want to know that when we see each other face-to-face, it's not going to be a test of wills. The manipulating and bribing have to stop."

"You're right."

"Why did you send the stained-glass window, then?"

"Because it's beautiful and I knew you'd love it. Why did you send it back?"

"Because it's beautiful, and I loved it."

"It doesn't go with my place."

She wanted badly to comment that nothing went with his place, but she held her tongue. "No more bribes."

"You say to-may-to, I say to-mah-to."

"Business. Period."

"All right, Lisa." The way he said her name with such sincerity and feeling hammered at her protective armor.

"I'm not kidding," she said and meant it.

"I know you're not. I agree to your terms. Thank you for calling, Lisa."

"We'll talk soon, then." She paused a moment too long. "Bye."

She hung up, satisfied with his promise but sorry

she'd had to wrest it out of him. No room for chances where Riley was concerned. Things needed to be as safe as she could make them. She was existing in a tissue-paper world—and it was raining.

The last thing Lisa wanted to do was attend the event at Town Hall on Saturday night of the next week. The Gold Fever Gala was being held in the huge reception room in the restored building. This evening had been planned in order to celebrate several things, including the boost to the economy and the production of gold from the Queen of Hearts, and to announce the plethora of projects which had been put in place.

As a popular Thunder Canyon daughter and the newly discovered heiress, Lisa had been invited as the guest of honor.

She had taken great care with her appearance, culling yet another divine red dress from the selection Gwen had pulled together for her. This one was calf length and slit up the side and left one shoulder bare. Tiny matching beads sewn on the fabric in leafy designs reflected the light.

A valet took Lisa's keys and the Blazer and parked it for her. Bernadine had offered to pick her up, but knowing her lawyer had a date, Lisa had refused.

Several people Lisa didn't know arrived just as she did. They introduced themselves and walked in through the double glass doors behind her.

Inside, the first person Lisa recognized was Emily Vaughn. She looked elegant in a deep-emerald gown that emphasized her sleek hair and dark eyes. Emily was quick to greet Lisa with a smile and a brief hug. "You look as though you're here for a roast."

"I'll try to compose myself. I'm still a novice at this social stuff. I expect to trip or sneeze on somebody's tie at any given minute."

"You're the woman of the hour, so try to relax and enjoy every minute while it lasts."

"I'll try. I feel like a big fake. I didn't do anything to be here. I'm only the mine owner because of my genes."

"Don't knock family money. Nobody ever says the Kennedys don't deserve what they have."

Lisa laughed. "I'll remember that."

A couple just inside the door to the reception hall greeted the two women. "Hi, Lisa. I'm Faith Stevenson, and this is my husband, Cam."

Lisa shook their hands. "Stevenson. You must be the parents of the boy who started this whole gold rush by falling into the mine."

Cam's brown eyes were as warm as his smile. "That's our claim to fame. It was scary, but it turned out well for everyone. Faith was the rescue worker who found Erik, and that's how we met."

"Well, congratulations. I'd love to meet Erik one of these days."

Bernadine was standing with Olivia Chester and a few other guests when Lisa spotted her. She gestured for Lisa to join them, and Emily excused herself and moved off into the crowd.

"You've met Olivia," Bernadine said.

"Hello again, Doctor."

"These are some of my colleagues." Olivia gestured to those beside her. "Christopher Taylor works in the E.R. and his wife, Zoe, is a resident."

"Nice to meet you."

"You, too," Zoe said. "I can see why red is your signature color. You look fabulous."

Lisa hadn't really thought of it like that. She'd chosen red dresses as a statement of pride about Lily, but she didn't mind the association. "Thank you."

The gathering broke up, and Lisa asked her lawyer, "Where's your date?"

"I thought he went to get drinks. I'd better go make sure he didn't meet someone else and forget about me."

More guests arrived and drinks flowed from bars set up in two corners of the room. Lisa was tickled to see Tildy Matheson had come to the reception. The woman was seated in an overstuffed chair, which had been situated for her comfort. Lisa pulled a folding chair close so they could visit.

"I already heard about the book project," Tildy told her. "Ben told me. I'm real proud of you for thinking of it. Catherine and Lily would be real proud, too."

"Thank you, Tildy. I'm grateful to you for helping me learn more about my ancestor."

Tildy glanced at the glass of wine a nearby guest held. "I could sure use a cup of tea. I don't suppose there's any to be had."

"I'll ask. You sit tight."

Lisa approached one of the corner bars. Two people

waiting in line moved aside so she could go first. "I'll wait my turn," she told them.

"Oh, no, you're the guest of honor. The guest of honor goes first."

"I just wanted to ask if there was any tea. Miss Matheson would like a cup."

"My wife carries a little tin with tea bags in her purse," the taller gentleman said. "I'll go ask her for one."

"They have a microwave in the back room," the other man said. "I'll go get a cup of hot water."

A few minutes later Lisa thanked them profusely and carried a mug of tea to Tildy.

"You're a dear girl," the old woman said. She blew on her tea and sipped it. "There's that nice Mark Anderson, the reporter who bought the *Nugget*."

Lisa glanced over at the dark-eyed man with graying hair at his temples. Bless Tildy for using the words *nice* and *reporter* in the same breath.

"He married that pretty Hispanic waitress from the Hitching Post, you know. He adopted her baby."

Lisa learned more local gossip at every event she attended. She could only imagine the speculation about her—and the talk regarding the times she'd been seen and photographed in Riley's company.

Justin and Katie Caldwell paused to greet the two women, and Lisa couldn't help glancing around for the rest of the Douglases. The room had grown full, and it was becoming more difficult to find people.

A ringing sound, like that of a glass being struck repeatedly with a utensil, resounded in the room and the crowd hushed.

Mayor Brookhurst stood on a podium, which had been set along one wall to elevate the speakers. "Attention, ladies and gentlemen! May I have your attention, please?"

Feedback from the microphone screeched and bystanders covered their ears.

Once the technical difficulties had been solved, the mayor proceeded. "Welcome one and all to our first Gold Fever Gala! Isn't this exciting? There hasn't been this much enthusiasm in Thunder Canyon for a good many years. I'm fortunate that the events of this year have taken place during my term. With everyone so happy and the town doing so well, maybe I'll get elected again just so I can bring good luck."

Soft laughter swept the crowd and a good-natured heckler told him democracy had nothing to do with luck.

"We're here tonight to celebrate our good fortune. The Queen of Hearts gold mine is in full production."

Applause rose in a resounding thunder.

"Our motels and restaurants, the gift shops, *all* the businesses have had more trade these past few months than in our history."

Residents clapped again.

"This evening there are several people we want to recognize for the parts they played in making this happen. We wanted to recognize Erik Stevenson's contribution, but his parents thought positive reinforcement for running away and hiding in the mine was a bad idea."

The crowd *Awww*ed collectively.

"But a donation to Erik's college fund is being made

on behalf of the Businessmen's Guild, and you're all sworn to secrecy until he's eighteen."

Lisa observed the smiles on Cam and Faith's faces. They hugged each other and went forward to accept the gift.

"This next award will be shared among several people who were each important in the events leading to our current boom. As you all know, Emily and Brad Vaughn were the ones who discovered the original deed to the mine. So, Emily and Brad, come up here beside me, please."

The couple made their way forward.

"Now, Brad and Emily wouldn't have come to Thunder Canyon at all if the Douglases hadn't paid for their investigation, so, Caleb and Riley, we want you in this group, too. Come on."

Murmurs went through the throng of guests. Caleb's silver hair came into view above the crowd, and then the rest of him as he stepped up onto the podium wearing his usual western-cut jacket. "Come on, Riley," he said.

Riley hung back and waved a dismissive hand. "I only wrote the checks. You found the team."

At his refusal to join them, Mayor Brookhurst went on. "Our next person of honor is the woman who kept the deed among her possessions for all these years until it could be claimed. Where's Matilda Matheson?"

A hubbub of chatter spread after her name was spoken, and after several minutes Tildy came forward, aided by Mark Anderson and Ben Saunders. They assisted her up to the platform. She was beaming with pleasure at the attention.

Riley lifted her chair into place, and she took a seat while the others stood beside her.

"Each of these fine people are hereby rewarded with a key to the city," the mayor said, and his assistant hung a large gold-foil key by a wide red ribbon around each of their necks.

Caleb looked at the mock key hanging on his shirt front and then aside as though he was sorry he'd come up for such pathetic praise.

"Now, that key doesn't really unlock anything," the mayor told them. "But whenever any of you want to be mayor for a day, you just bring your key to the Hall and the job is yours."

Laughter rippled through the crowd, and everyone clapped for those being honored. After pictures were taken, they dispersed back into the cluster of guests.

"Let *me* be mayor for a day and he'd never get hired again," Caleb said as an aside, and he received a few sidelong glances.

Oblivious to the comment, the mayor resumed his task. "Last but certainly not least, we have a special guest of honor we want to recognize right now. The people of Thunder Canyon want this young lady to know we're proud of her. Come on up here, please, Lisa Jane Martin!"

Lisa felt the warmth of nervousness climb her neck and face. This public recognition was so out of her element that if it had happened a month ago, she would have fainted dead away. She'd gained self-confidence in that month, however, and she was no longer ashamed of her connection to her great-great-grandmother. She held her head high and walked through the crowd.

Phil Wagner happened to be standing nearest, so he reached for her hand to help her. She held her skirt and stepped up on the riser.

Cameras snapped and whirred.

"Lisa, as owner of the Queen of Hearts, you've already shown that you're going to give back to our community. As docent of the museum, Ben Saunders is going to talk about the book project for the historical society."

Ben did indeed get up and share the details of the book he was authoring and that Lisa was publishing. "What we hope to do with this project is dispel the myths that have surrounded Lily all these years and present the facts. I'm honored that Lisa has asked me to do this."

After he stepped down and the applause quieted, the mayor looked at Lisa with a big smile. "We have another surprise to share. One of Lisa's first business ventures will be the Claim Jumper restaurant. Fine dining right here in Thunder Canyon."

The excitement over the announcements abated momentarily.

"In recognition, Lisa, we present you with this." He turned to where his assistant held out a box with the lid removed. From inside, Mayor Brookhurst took a gold tiara set with heart-shaped stones.

A few bystanders chuckled, but everyone clapped enthusiastically.

"You are now—officially—the queen of our hearts."

Smiling, Lisa stood still so he could place the tiara on her head, securing the combs in her hair.

Among the sea of faces, she spotted Bernadine smiling and clapping. Her date was a handsome fellow with a mustache and slightly graying hair.

Lisa's gaze locked with Riley's then, and the noise of the room faded away. Queen of their hearts was lovely. But she'd like to have a place in one special person's heart.

Congratulations were effusive, and she lost sight of Riley. She posed for pictures with the mayor and the other honorees.

An awkward hush caught Lisa's attention. It became clear that someone was saying something that had made people stop and listen.

Standing only five feet away with his hands in his pockets, Caleb Douglas rocked back on his heels. His next words were clear. "Why, she's probably the only trailer-trash royalty in the state of Montana."

No one laughed. His derogatory remark dampened the frivolous mood and garnered more than a few stares. A dozen sidelong glances were cast at Lisa to see if she'd overheard.

Her ears burned with anger. She wasn't ashamed of who she was or where she'd come from. It was the fact that he'd belittled her heritage and her family that got her feathers in a snit.

She turned a glare on him that would have scorched a lesser man. "I may not have been raised in a fancy house and waited on hand and foot," she told him. "But my grandmother and my aunt loved me and they taught me honesty and integrity. I wouldn't use another person's feelings to get what I want, and I would never encourage a child of mine to do the same."

Caleb seemed surprised by her show of grit and the way people had listened to what she had to say.

"I think that crown's gone to your head, missy," he said. "Just like the money did."

This wasn't the time or the place to vent her hurt and anger over the Douglases' manipulations, so she took a breath and counted to ten. Ten wasn't enough. She opened her mouth to speak, but before anything came out, Riley's voice interrupted her.

"Lisa's the last person who would let money go to her head," he said, speaking directly to his father. "She's the most genuine, unaffected and trustworthy person I know. That you could have anything ugly to say about her tells me you don't know her. If you did, you'd know someone with a lot of love to give and very little concern about what money will get her."

Riley turned, and Lisa met his vivid green gaze. His attention refocused on her.

"If you knew her," he continued, "you'd have to love her."

Lisa's heart staggered and she took several deliberate breaths to make sure she didn't pass out. This was worse than sneezing on someone's tie, but she didn't really care. She wanted to hear what he had to say.

"I got to know her," Riley said. "And now I can't think about anything else but loving her."

Tears welled up and clung to Lisa's lower lashes until she saw him through a watery blur.

Riley turned to the people beside him, as though explaining to a jury. "I deceived her when we met. I pretended to be interested in her when I was really only concerned about regaining ownership of the gold mine. My values were nothing you'd want to teach your children."

"What about now?" Heads turned to discover the voice that had spoken that question belonged to Adele Douglas, looking cool and sophisticated as always in a stunning silver dress. The crowd parted for her to move closer to her son. "What are you concerned with now, Riley?"

He glanced from his mother back to Lisa. "I'm concerned with convincing her I can change." His gaze was warm and beseeching. "With showing her I deserve a second chance."

"And?" Adele asked softly.

"And with proving that my love for her is real."

Lisa's blood pounded through her veins.

"I love you, Lisa," he said. "Please forgive me. Please marry me. Please…give me another chance."

In the silence that followed, you could have heard an itch. No one seemed to breathe as anticipation and hope electrified the room.

Lisa couldn't take her focus from Riley's face. His cheeks were high with color, but his eyes were pleading and sincere. She knew people were watching and waiting on all sides and she could imagine the look on Caleb's face, but none of that mattered at this moment.

The most unexpected image came to her unbidden. At that moment she saw Lily Divine's face as it appeared in her photographs and in the painting. Her great-great-grandmother's smile of contentment made Lisa yearn to share Lily's peace with her life choices. Made her desire the same assurance that she was being all she could be and leaving no breathing room for regrets.

Lisa's nerves had calmed and she was thinking with perfect rationality. She had no guarantee that Riley wasn't pulling the ultimate scam right at this moment. That he hadn't staged this for her benefit or even that his father hadn't been a part of it. But she didn't think so.

At last Lisa's gaze faltered and shot to Caleb where he stood. His face was red with anger and his green eyes shot lethal daggers at her. If he was in on a scheme, he would be much more pulled together and look less as if he would burst a blood vessel in his forehead at any moment.

Riley's expression didn't seem quite as confident as it would if he thought he'd pulled a fast one. In fact, she thought he'd begun to look decidedly anxious.

"I'll sign a prenuptial agreement," he told her, uncannily zeroing in on her last uncertainty.

"I can have one drawn up in five minutes." Bernadine's voice had come from several feet away. Her suggestion released the crowd's tension, and laughter rippled.

Lisa took several steps forward until she stood within an arm's length of Riley. "There aren't any guarantees," she said. "A hundred years ago someone bought a claim to the land where the mine sits, with nothing more than hope as a guide. Then somewhere along the line another somebody gave up. The gold was in there all along."

"I know this is a long-winded metaphor for something, Lisa, but could you speed it up and tell me how it turns out?" Riley asked.

She grinned. "It turns out that some things happen by chance. Like Erik stumbling into the mine. Like me being related to Lily."

"*Maybe* it's chance," Riley said. "But maybe it's not. Maybe there's a time and a reason for everything."

"Isn't that a Simon and Garfunkel song?"

"Not exactly."

She took a step forward and placed her hand on his arm. "In any case, I'd rather take my chances with love—and trust. I don't want any regrets."

Riley slipped his arm around her shoulders. "I'll see that you don't have any."

"You'd better make your second chance good."

"This time I love you."

She raised on her toes to meet his kiss. Riley wrapped his arms around her, and she clung to him greedily. She was never going to let go of this man again.

Around them the crowd cheered and whistled.

Lisa was so filled with joy, she could barely breathe. When the kiss ended, she glanced around at the smiles and tears on the faces of the people of Thunder Canyon. She had misjudged a lot of these people. And some of them had misjudged her, as well. She was big on second chances.

A movement caught her eye. Caleb had turned toward the door, and his wife watched as Justin and Katie broke away from the others to follow him.

"Your father hates me."

"Like I said, he doesn't even know you."

"I don't want to come between you."

"Right now there are a few value issues between us. If he wants to salvage his family, he'll come around. I'm not changing. And I'm not giving you up. Not for anything." His gaze rose to her hair. "You're the queen of my heart, too."

She remembered the tiara on her head. "What do you suppose the headlines will say tomorrow?" She glanced around. "Is Chad Falkner here?"

Riley gestured with a thumb over his shoulder. "Saw him back there. Why?"

"I'm wondering if *People* magazine will put my picture beside Queen Latifah's this time."

"Who?"

"Never mind. You're really going to have to widen your interests and take in a few movies."

"I'll take you all the time."

"We could open a theater! Or an old-fashioned drive-in. Wouldn't that be fun?"

"So, you'll marry me?"

"Yes!"

He squeezed her hand and smiled.

"I'm having my house moved, you know."

"I'll live there with you."

"Will you *not* bring your furniture?"

"How about my bed?"

"Okay, your bed. We'll need room for the boys."

Riley groaned.

Lisa laughed and he crushed her in a hug.

"Montana Woman Has Big Plans. My house at eleven."

"Local Heiress Gives Thunder Canyon Scion A Second Chance," he said against her ear. "Montana man has never been happier, and it has nothing to do with gold."

Epilogue

Lisa glanced around their new backyard—well, *acreage,* actually. Riley had convinced her to have her grandmother's house moved to this incredible forested site near a stream on a northeast section of Douglas land with a breathtaking view of the mountains.

No longer did she need dog runs to cage her beloved boys while she was away. This entire section of land had been fenced in so they could run for half an acre and back.

Today the area directly outside the back door was set up with enormous canopies and long tables in preparation for their housewarming party. The celebration had been Katie's idea, and she waddled between the kitchen, the two caterers' vans and the tables, making sure everything was arranged perfectly.

She and Lisa had announced their pregnancies at nearly the same time. Katie's baby was due in eleven weeks and Lisa's in ten. Lisa was delighted that her child would grow up with a cousin so close in age, an aunt and an uncle and even grandparents. This was the family she'd always wanted, even if some of the relationships still needed a little work.

The side gate opened and Justin and Riley carried flat boxes toward the tables.

"What're those?" Lisa called.

"More cakes," Riley answered. "The baker at Super Saver Mart wanted to contribute something to the festivities, so she made these this morning."

"Goodness," Katie said. "We already had four cakes."

"Don't worry that they'll go to waste," Justin told his wife. "Riley invited all the store employees and their families to stop by this afternoon."

Lisa laughed and gave her husband a hug, which was becoming more difficult with the size of her belly coming between them. Riley rested a hand atop her stomach and kissed her. "How's little Frodo doing?"

"His name's not Frodo," Lisa replied. After they'd watched the entire *Lord of the Rings* series together, he'd become obsessed with naming their expected child after one of the characters. Last week it had been Aragorn.

"You can name our next pet Frodo, not our child. We could agree on Sam," she told him for the hundredth time.

Excited barks sounded, and Riley stepped away from her to greet Joey, Piper and Derek. Derek had stayed with them a few months ago when Riley's father had been in the hospital for bypass surgery, and now Adele brought the poodle at least once a week for a sleepover. She claimed he needed the exercise and companionship, and Lisa's two retrievers were used to new canines sharing their space.

Riley knelt and gave each dog equal attention, scratching behind their ears and stroking their fur. He'd convinced his mother to let Derek's fur grow out of the ridiculous pom-pom cut.

"I told you this canine has more dignity and self-respect now," he said.

Lisa and Katie shared a look.

"What?" he said defensively. "Look at him. He's one of the guys now."

"He's no different, Riley," Katie told him. "Only his appearance has changed."

"Improved appearance does bring confidence," Lisa said.

"Are you people talking about the dog?" Justin asked.

Riley gave Derek a solid pat on the haunches and stood. "Lisa told me once that Derek only has so many years in him, so I'd better make the most of them."

"I guess that's true about anything," Justin said. "Like you and I, Riley. We don't have a past as family, but you've let me into your present and future."

Riley looked at his half brother. "Your birth wasn't your fault. I always understood that. I don't know what I resented more—the fact that our father was deceptive or that you forgave him so easily."

"I wanted a family," Justin replied. "More than I wanted to hang on to the anger."

The conversation had turned more serious, and the two couples glanced at each other.

"Riley's letting the Derek philosophy spill over to Caleb," Lisa said.

Riley nodded. "Seeing him in the hospital showed me we didn't have a lifetime to work through this stuff, so we need to do it now."

"Did he tell you he was sorry?" Katie asked. "It's tough to forgive when someone isn't sorry."

"Not in so many words," Riley answered with a shrug. "Right off I made it plain how things would be regarding my wife. He didn't know Lisa and he was judging her unfairly. Everything has always been about money with him."

Riley studied his beautiful wife, her eyes bright with the pleasure of life. Tiny ringlets of hair lay against her cheeks and temples. She bothered less and less to straighten it these days, but it didn't matter. She was all the more beautiful carrying his child.

"Once, it was all about money with me, too." He took her hand and brought it to his lips. "Until I found out money really can't buy love or happiness."

"Sure helped with all the extras, though." Lisa smiled and touched his cheek.

"I missed a lot by not looking outside my narrow, moneyed life," he said. "Thank goodness I had another chance."

"*We* have a second chance," she corrected.

Justin wrapped his arm around his wife's shoulder and they strolled away from the couple who'd become absorbed in each other.

Piper barked at a squirrel and the three dogs bounded away.

"I have a surprise for you." He took a red velvet ring box from his pocket and opened it before showing her what lay inside.

Lisa took the plain gold band between her thumb and forefinger. "It's beautiful, Riley! But I already have a wedding ring."

"It's not a wedding ring. It's made from some of the first gold mined from the Queen of Hearts. It's just…a symbol."

None of this would have happened if gold hadn't been found or if Lisa hadn't been proven the rightful owner. For once, losing had turned out to be the best thing that had ever happened to Riley Douglas.

Lisa slipped the ring on a finger and kissed him.

Her kisses were better than anything money could buy.

* * * * *

Coming in July from

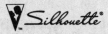

SPECIAL EDITION™

A tale of love, pizza and the lottery

TICKET TO LOVE
by Jen Safrey

New York waitress Acey Corelli is *sure* she knows the identity of the winner of an unclaimed $35-million lottery—Harry Wells, a sexy cowboy working as a writer. Acey decides to help Harry conquer his fears and claim his prize. Little does she know that Harry *is* already a millionaire, a runaway ranching heir from Texas. An undeniable attraction begins.... Sometimes you just can't fight fate.

Available at your favorite retail outlet.
On sale July 2005.

Where love comes alive™

If you enjoyed what you just read,
then we've got an offer you can't resist!

Take 2 bestselling
love stories FREE!
Plus get a FREE surprise gift!

Clip this page and mail it to Silhouette Reader Service™

IN U.S.A.	**IN CANADA**
3010 Walden Ave.	P.O. Box 609
P.O. Box 1867	Fort Erie, Ontario
Buffalo, N.Y. 14240-1867	L2A 5X3

YES! Please send me 2 free Silhouette Special Edition® novels and my free surprise gift. After receiving them, if I don't wish to receive anymore, I can return the shipping statement marked cancel. If I don't cancel, I will receive 6 brand-new novels every month, before they're available in stores! In the U.S.A., bill me at the bargain price of $4.24 plus 25¢ shipping and handling per book and applicable sales tax, if any*. In Canada, bill me at the bargain price of $4.99 plus 25¢ shipping and handling per book and applicable taxes**. That's the complete price and a savings of at least 10% off the cover prices—what a great deal! I understand that accepting the 2 free books and gift places me under no obligation ever to buy any books. I can always return a shipment and cancel at any time. Even if I never buy another book from Silhouette, the 2 free books and gift are mine to keep forever.

235 SDN DZ9D
335 SDN DZ9E

Name	(PLEASE PRINT)	
Address	Apt.#	
City	State/Prov.	Zip/Postal Code

Not valid to current Silhouette Special Edition® subscribers.

Want to try two free books from another series?
Call 1-800-873-8635 or visit www.morefreebooks.com.

* Terms and prices subject to change without notice. Sales tax applicable in N.Y.
** Canadian residents will be charged applicable provincial taxes and GST.
   All orders subject to approval. Offer limited to one per household.
   ® are registered trademarks owned and used by the trademark owner and or its licensee.

SPED04R   ©2004 Harlequin Enterprises Limited